SNEAKIN'

AND

FREAKIN'

with my Professor

SNEAKIN' AND FREAKIN' WITH MY PROFESSOR

BY

M. MONIQUE

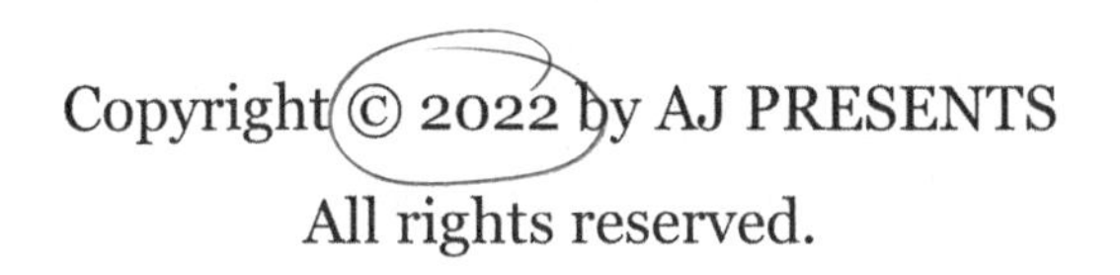

This book is a work of fiction. Names, characters, places, and incidents either are products of the author's imagination or are used fictitiously. Any resemblance to actual persons, living or dead, events, or locales is entirely coincidental.

The Cataloging-in-Publication Data is on file at the Library of Congress.

AJPRESENTS

Printed in the United States of America

10 9 8 7 6 5 4 3 2 1

PROLOGUE

MILA DASH

Weddings made my ass itch. But I was here to support my best friend, Kai, on her day. If "grin and bear it" was a person, she was me. There wasn't any major or deep reason for why I hated weddings other than the fact that I couldn't get a man to be serious enough with me for a simple relationship let alone a marriage.

Case in point, my boyfriend Amir, heavy on the boy, sat in the second pew, acting aggravated as hell that he had to be here with me. I invited him to see if it would actually touch something in his brain to make him see that this was the end game. We'd been together for almost a year now, and he had yet to bring up anything resembling a marriage.

I guess I shouldn't be surprised. Amir was good to look at, but mentally, he and I were on two different levels. While I had my five-year plan in place, Amir wasn't thinking about anything but the next few minutes.

We met at Kai's sister's graduation party. He was there supporting his brother who'd also just graduated from high school. Amir was fine as hell and charming, drawing me in with his white smile. Our first conversation turned into us going on our first date.

A year later, we were still in the same place we started. I wasn't sure what we were anymore. I called him my boyfriend when really, he was more like my roommate. Sex between us wasn't hitting on anything these days. According to my other best friend, Lucy, because Amir wasn't meeting my needs emotionally and mentally, having sex with him had become a chore rather than being pleasurable.

I agreed with Lucy, though. That's the only reason that could explain why I stood here staring at a complete stranger. It wasn't so much that I was staring than the fact that he had my skin on fire from the way he stared back.

Lord, he was saying something to me with those brown eyes of his. The devilish twinkle in them didn't make it any better. If he smirked at me one more time, I was going to ask the pastor to stop the ceremony so that I could run to the restroom. I'd never had a man ogle me in a way that made me hot all over. As if he could smell my essence leaving my body, he bit into his lip and flashed me a smile that sent my mind straight to the gutter. This moment seemed so intimate.

Breaking eye contact, I pretended as if I heard everything the pastor said and smiled.

After the nuptials were complete, I lagged behind while the wedding pictures were being taken. Amir's face balled up as he approached me.

"How much longer we gon' be here?" he asked.

Sarcastically smiling at his handsome face, I said, "You're free to go back to the hotel, Amir. I'll have Lucy and Darren give me a lift."

His mug deepened. "Nah, yeen ridin' nowhere with them. I feel like that nigga playin' in my face and I'on like that," he said.

Now my face was balled up.

Amir wrapped his arms around me and explained, "He got all the opps here."

I busted out laughing just as he appeared in my peripheral vision.

"Damn, shawty," he drawled. Unashamed, his eyes tumbled down my body.

He was tall as hell, even taller than Amir's six feet. His broad shoulders and hard chest strained against his button-down in the most delicious way. The tattoo covering the expanse of his neck looked like something demonic.

Delicious would be his dark, brown skin. I wondered if his thick beard was soft or kinky to the touch. His scent captivated me which was crazy since he smelled heavily of marijuana.

"You're one beautiful ass woman," he praised.

My mouth slightly fell at his boldness. Amir looked between the two of us like I knew this man.

Amir's arms fell from around me as he stepped in the man's face. "Aye, bruh-"

"Be glad I'm in a good mood," he stated, interrupting Amir, but keeping his eyes on me. My eyes stretched.

"Yeah, we're definitely glad you're in a good mood, Grim" Darren interjected as he came between Amir and who I now knew to be Grim.

Grim as in, Darren's cousin, Grim? This was the man Darren and Kai's husband, Chuck, referred to whenever they mentioned going to "work"? I'd heard his name a few times, curious as to why anyone would walk around calling themselves such a crazy ass name.

Grim smirked at Amir and gave me another scathing once over before walking away with Darren. I hated to say I watched the way he walked, mesmerized by the fit of his black slacks, and the bow of his designer covered feet.

"I'm ready to fuckin' go, mane. These niggas gon' make me air this bitch out."

I rolled my eyes back Amir's way. "Air what out, Amir?" He was always threatening to shoot somebody.

He smacked his teeth. "Just hurry up, so we can go."

While he stalked off to go sit back down, I waved him off, and went on about my business.

Two years later...

"Yes, mama, I'm settling in fine."

"Are you sure, Mila? I don't like you being so far away from us."

My mama was on the phone being dramatic as hell. She and my dad helped me move two weeks ago, and I swear, every five minutes she was calling me.

Snickering, I replied, "Mama you're forty-five minutes up the road."

"Yeah, but what if you need a babysitter?"

"A babysitter?" I croaked. "Mama, I don't have a child or a man to create one with why in the world do I need a babysitter? And if I did, Kai and Lucy are here."

Mama grumbled. "He wasn't it for you anyway, baby. Sometimes people get moved out of your life-"

"Mama, no, okay. It's not that I still care, because I'm over Amir. But I don't want to rehash the situation." I hated when she brought up Amir. He was another failed relationship that reminded me of why I needed to stay my ass single. If she knew Amir was the reason for why I'd moved, she wouldn't dare be bringing his name up.

"Which is how you know he wasn't for you. There's no way in hell you'd be "over" a man that you're in love with. Not this soon."

This soon meaning ten months after our breakup. Frankly, the last ten months had been hell. Being stalked by an ex wasn't the life.

"It's been long enough," I answered.

"Like I said, there's no way. I've been married to your daddy for almost thirty years, and he gets on my last nerve."

I chuckled.

"But I'd never get over him should anything happen to us. He's the love of my life."

"I know, ma," I sighed. She reminded me too often how much in love she and my dad were. It was evident whether she voiced her feelings or not.

"Can we change the subject?" I asked.

She smacked her teeth. "Send me pictures of your office once you're done decorating."

Now that made me smile.

"Of course, mama. I'm glad Mrs. Jackie was able to squeeze me in somewhere."

"Jackie loves you like she birthed you, Mila," she chuckled. "The minute I told her you were relocating to Pensacola, she was excited. Dean of the English department is a mighty big title, but I know my baby girl can do the job with ease."

Filled with pride, I smiled. "Not for a few more months, Ma. I'm covering for another professor until he returns."

"Yes, but your title still is Dean, dear," she said. "You're a young, black woman who's going to be head of her department at a historically black university. That's an honor, and a big deal. I hope you're treating it as such."

Nodding, I replied, "I am."

"Your dad and I couldn't be prouder of you."

I was proud of me too. At twenty-nine I'd accomplished more than I could've imagined as far as my career was concerned. Being offered a dean's position after serving as a professor for five years was honorable. Even after taking a short break, being back in my field is exactly where I needed to be to get my mind off other irrelevant subjects—like being single and lonely as fuck.

Being single wouldn't be so bad if my mind wasn't consumed with images of a man who had broad shoulders and beautiful brown eyes. My senses wouldn't be craving the smell of marijuana and... Chanel.

Grim.

Imagine hearing a man's name mentioned for the past two years and you could do nothing but hear his voice telling you how sexy he thought you were. That's what I'd been living. I hadn't seen Grim since the wedding, but I couldn't make my mind let him loose.

"Although I'm sad you're in another city, I feel like this move is good for you," my mom said.

"Me too," I agreed.

I had my best friends to help keep me focused, and my career to keep me busy. My life was indeed looking up.

All smiles, I waved and spoke as students filed into my lecture hall the following Monday morning. Curious, many stared. I took it in stride knowing if it wasn't for the khaki, ankle-cropped skinny pants, cream silk blouse, navy blue fitted blazer, and same color pumps on my feet, I would seamlessly fit right in.

"Oh, muthafuckin' goodness."

At the sound of his voice, my entire body froze.

Grim strode my way, surprised, but smiling from ear to ear.

I don't know what the hell he said. I was too busy cussing myself out.

CHAPTER 1

MILA DASH

2 Months Later...

Good morning, my professor. I was wondering if you had time to explain this latest article you assigned. I'm free any time. -Grim

Pure heat assailed my soul seeing Spade Graham's name on the header of this damn email. This man right here was on my last nerve. I'd been a professor for five years and never in that time had I ran into a student as obnoxious as Mr. Graham.

Three more weeks, Mila.

I coached myself because that is all that I could do. My time as his professor wouldn't be over soon enough.

It was hard trying to avoid eye contact with him, especially when he commanded the room as if he was the only one there. His tall frame had to reach every bit of six-foot-five-inches, and trust me, he wore his height like a well-fitted condom. WTF?! Despite the size of my classroom, Mr. Graham managed to have the only distinct scent. Twice a week I was forced to smell his Chanel cologne coupled with blunt he'd smoked prior to class.

What I disliked most about this pupil was the face God painted on him. His milk chocolate, blemish-free face was literally perfect, even with the beard he sported. Brown eyes that followed my every step were seated underneath a healthy array of enviable lashes and thick eyebrows. His nose was that of a warrior, and his lips were magnificently thick.

"You know this is fate, right?" he asked, approaching my desk after class ended.

Flustered, I stuttered over my words. "What're you talking about?" I knew exactly what he was talking about. However, I couldn't play into Spade's game. Not only were my other students tuned in to see what our exchange was about, but I couldn't be caught dead flirting with this man.

"First of all, I didn't know you were in my city. Second, out of all the professors that could've been chosen to cover for

Professor Mason, it's you." His eyes scorched my body as they traveled down my figure.

"See you Wednesday, Mr. Graham," I urged.

He smirked and cocked his head. "Oh, I get it," he said. "Sure thing, my professor."

Damn. What did I do to deserve the punishment of being around such a handsome man?

A year ago, I was happily broken up with my ex, Amir. He'd cheated on me one time and that was all it took for me to chuck him the deuces. I thought that would be the end of him, however, he found the gall to start stalking me.

The stalking got so bad that I started making excuses for why I needed to stay the night at my parents' house. Neither of them questioned anything. And as crazy as Amir thought he was, he knew my dad was by far crazier.

So, he did other stupid shit, like sending me flowers to my workplace, to waiting for me in the parking lot. He'd never exhibited stalking behavior before, which admittedly had my ass terrified of him. I stopped working and everything, feigning burn out.

Amir's stalking calmed down after that point. However, he still found some way to disrupt my peace. It wasn't until I moved to Pensacola that I found some true peace. I wasn't sure if Amir knew where I was or not, and as long as he left me the hell alone, I was fine with that.

Somehow running from Amir pushed me right into Spade Graham's path.

Professor Mason, the professor who normally taught Spade's class, had a family emergency which caused him to step away from his position. He'd be returning in three weeks to resume his post. These three damn weeks wouldn't speed past fast enough.

Coming to work for Robert Monroe University was easily the best decision I'd made in a very long time. The school's rich history was one that made anyone proud to be a part of the community. Not only that, but my mother's best friend, Mrs. Jackie, who was RMUs senior administrative officer, checked in on me often. She made it her business to make sure I was enjoying my time here. Although I'd only been here two months, I felt at home.

Yes, I felt at home. And Spade Graham wasn't going to ruin that.

Mr. Graham, you aced the last assignment the class was given. I find it hard to comprehend why you would need help on this assignment. Both assignments are along the same lines. If you are truly stuck, then I would not mind setting aside a few minutes tomorrow.

-Professor Dash

I sent the return email and sighed. Completing the rest of my emails was a breeze as none of my other students rattled me like Mr. Graham.

Now that I knew his real name, I was curious as to why he chose to be called Grim. If I took a wild guess, it wasn't because he was sweet and harmless. Spade had *that* look—the one that made niggas think twice about crossing him in any way. His smile was easy, but I could see straight through it. Spade wasn't a man to play with.

I had to remind myself that he was related to my best friend's husband. While I was over here being professor of the year, my best friends were busy being housewives to two of the biggest kingpins in the south. While Kai and Lucy should have juicy stories to tell about their lives, they were so far removed from their husbands' work, that they were as boring as me.

As far as I was told, Spade was a club owner. It figured that he spent his time around women the way he garnered attention. Although he wore nothing more than joggers, t-shirts, and sneakers, he oozed wealth, arrogance, and confidence like nobody's business.

Every woman in the lecture hall waited for him to come to class just to lay eyes on him. I couldn't blame them one bit.

But... Spade made it well-known that he wanted me. Whether it was from him blocking every other male student from getting my attention or finding his way to my desk every fifteen minutes. While I loathed his presence, I was proud of witnessing a black man pursue higher education, so I did my best to have patience.

I'd barely sent Spade the email when he responded back.

Growling, I clicked the open button.

I'm stuck. What time may I come by?

-Grim

My fingers dug into the keys of my laptop as I wrote him back. Not only did he ace his last paper, but Spade was sitting comfortably at the top of the class. Shaking my head, I gave him a time and told him not to be late as I had other shit to do.

He'd just seen me this morning, trailing my every move with his bedroom eyes. Because of him, every class I wore outfits that didn't show too much of my shape although it was difficult to conceal it without looking like an old lady. No matter how low I thought my fitted blazers were cut, I'd still feel Spade starring at my ass.

See you then, my professor.

-Grim

My eyes narrowed at his little *my professor* line. I'd told him once to stop calling me that shit, but apparently, he didn't take direction well.

*****

"You're coming tomorrow night, and that's the end of discussion."

I mugged the phone and rolled my eyes. Kai was on my phone trying to talk me into coming with her and Lucy to this new club that had opened downtown.

Kai and I had been friends for years. She moved here to Pensacola, Florida years ago, while I chose to stay in our hometown Mobile, Alabama.

"Kai, you can't force me go somewhere I don't want to. I planned on spending my Friday night—"

"Lonely as fuck," Kai blurted.

Smacking my teeth, I replied, "*Minding my business.*"

"Mila," she groaned. "For the past three years it's the same thing. Even when you had a man you spent your birthday lonely as hell. Amari was off doing him not giving a fuck about you. As your very married best friend, I'm telling you, you need to get your ass out, and live a little."

Clearing my throat past the thick clog of regret I felt, I said, "My birthday isn't until next weekend. That has nothing to do with tomorrow night, Kai. And besides, I don't want to visit a club where *he* will surely be."

Her deep sigh met my ears. "Grim will hardly notice us there, boo, since it's his grand opening. Tomorrow night you're supposed to bring your ass out so you can find a damn man to spend your birthday with. Mila, you're a professor, so playing stupid with me isn't gonna work. Should I call Lucy?"

"Hell no," I griped. Kai and I met Lucy eight years back at a house party we attended. Lucy was the crazy one of the three of us.

"So, do I need to pick you up, or you're meeting us there?"

Sighing, I pinched the bridge of my nose and said, "Pick me up, damn, Kai."

She laughed and hooted. "And where some sexy shit! Show off that body you got, boo!"

"Bye, Kai," I hung up just as there was a knock at my office door. Checking the time, my heart raced knowing it was Spade on the other side.

"Come in," I croaked, mad at the unexpected catch in my voice.

The door cracked open, revealing his overpowering frame, and bringing in his ratchet ass scent. Today, he had a hat propped on top of his low-cut hair. Behind my desk, I had to cross my legs when he smiled.

"Hey, my professor," he politely spoke and took the chair across from me. He barely fit in it. Shit, I had to avert my gaze, wishing he wouldn't wear sweats around me. His print left absolutely nothing to the imagination.

"Mr. Graham," I chided.

"I know, my fault, my professor. It's hard callin' you Professor Dash. I'on like that shit."

My well-arched eyebrows lifted in question.

"I'd call you, Mrs. Graham, though" he stated.

I turned my nose up while my middle danced in my jeans.

"Mr. Graham," I warned.

He chuckled and shrugged. "Aight," he acquiesced. "Could you at least call me Grim since we're in private?"

"I'm never calling you that name, Mr. Graham."

He chuckled. "Never say never, baby."

Ready to get this over with, I asked, "What are you stuck on?" I noticed he came in my office without so much as a book, let alone a notebook.

He didn't readily answer me. Instead, he stared at me.

"Well?" I prompted.

"I'ain stuck," he admitted. "I just have a question for you."

Leaning back in my chair, I crossed my arms over my breast and studied his arrogant ass.

"You're wasting my time," I said after a minute had passed.

"I'd never waste ya time, beautiful."

"Mr.—"

"Yeah, I know," he backtracked. He smoothed his hand down his thick, black beard and continued to stare.

Feeling his gaze penetrate through my blazer, I prompted him again. "What is your question, Mr. Graham?"

He leaned forward and rested his elbows on his thighs, then cocked his head at me.

"Do you find me attractive?"

I busted out laughing as I stood to go to my door.

"Alright, Mr. Graham. This is where I ask you to leave." He was dead ass serious, and for some reason that made me nervous. As I turned the doorknob to open the door, he was swiftly in front of me halting me. While I should've been scared or at least intimidated by his move and the fact that he loomed over me like a giant sequoia, instead I felt...

Hell no!

I wondered if he could hear my heart beating out of my chest.

"It's a simple question, Professor."

His already deep voice turned into something I'd hear in my dreams for nights to come. It didn't help that I'd woken up to sweaty nights because of him. I hated to admit that even while I was with Amir, dreams of Spade would sometimes visit me. At first, I was ashamed of dreaming about another man. As time passed and my relationship with Amir soured, I looked forward to going to sleep, hoping Spade would show his face.

Two years of dreaming and now Spade was standing in front of me, looking like he wanted to hem me up against this door. He was standing too close, close enough for his scent to wrap itself around me.

"The weed you're wearing is giving me a headache." That's all I could think to say.

He smirked. "Just tell me I smell good, baby."

"If you did, I wouldn't be fighting a headache right now," I countered.

"I got somethin' for that," he quickly responded.

Clearing my throat, I glanced away before I drowned in his eyes.

"You gon' answer my question?"

I shook my head, and again, tried to turn the knob.

"Do I need security to make you leave, Mr. Graham?"

He smiled, showing off his glistening white teeth. "Sure, call 'em," he provoked.

Leaving the door, I stalked back to my desk prepared to call security.

"If you'd let me, I'd be swallowin' ya pleasure before they arrive."

His comment had me pausing in my tracks. My hand stilled on the phone as my eyes flew to his frame coming towards me. This time when he crowded my space, his hand came up to cup my cheek. Was it crazy that his hand literally swallowed my face? I held my breath as he trailed his fingers down the side of my face and along my neck until his hand softly gripped the back of my neck. My nipples pebbled against my bra as goosebumps prickled my skin.

Bending down, his lips softly touched my forehead in a gentle kiss causing me to die a little on the inside. His lips felt exactly how they looked.

"You're sexy as fuck, my professor. How many times I gotta tell you that before you understand how fuckin' bad I want you? I wanna do unspeakable shit to you—all good, or all bad dependin' on how you take it."

I wasn't sure if he was referring to that thing poking me in my abdomen, or my actual thought process. Lifting my head to meet his gaze and give him a stern look, I was taken aback when his lips brushed against mine.

"If you knew how I felt about kissin', you wouldn't look at my lips like that." Sexily, he tugged at his bottom lip.

A knock at my office door had me jumping out of my skin. Spade, however, didn't budge.

"Mr. Graham-"

"Grim," he corrected.

I mugged him. "I'm not calling you that," I reiterated.

His fingers gliding across my lips had me knocking his hand away. "Mr. Graham, please. I can't...we can't do this. Will you leave?"

He slowly licked his lips and nodded. As he stepped away, his gaze slid over my body.

"You're still my professor," he informed me.

Huffing, I pointed to the door. As he opened the door, in sailed Sullivan, a professor I'd gotten to know since starting here. He was handsome with his light skin and perfect light brown eyes. He too was tall and commanded attention while in a room. Sullivan wasn't as broad as Spade; however, he was lean and cut with pristine. He and Spade eyed each other, with Spade grinning in Sullivan's face, taunting him.

"Can I help you?" I asked Professor Sullivan, snatching his gaze from Spade who stood at the door ear hustling like my business was his. "I'll see you in class Monday," I told Spade. He gave Sullivan what seemed to be a warning glare before leaving.

Mr. Sullivan chuckled. "You know that's not a good look," he stated.

"Please," I held up my hand, "nothing's even like that. That's the last thing my mind is on." The lies I tell!

"Good, because it would go against the university's policy to fraternize with students. You're new here, so I wouldn't want you to get caught up breaking the rules." He chuckled. "Trust me, I know it can be difficult."

Side-eyeing him, I could only imagine what his thought process was when he saw an attractive female student. My thoughts were probably PG related to his. That wasn't my business, though.

"You don't need to tell me," I reiterated. "The same policies state there shouldn't be any fraternizing amongst colleagues."

He didn't have a comeback for that one. He smiled instead.

I sat behind my desk and began cleaning it, so that I could go home and start my weekend. Fridays were my off days and, if it weren't for Kai, I'd be knee deep in a book this weekend instead of going to some raggedy club with her and Lucy.

Who was I kidding? Any club owned by Spade Graham wasn't raggedy. I hadn't been to his other club, but I heard the stories of how nice it was.

"Who follows those rules anyhow?" Mr. Sullivan asked bringing me out of my thoughts. To that I laughed.

"Hypocrite," I drawled. "Is there something you needed?" Sullivan was handsome, and he knew it. Having a woman fall at his feet was as simple as snapping his fingers. Unlike Spade, Sullivan didn't rattle my nerves. He was one of those guys that was just handsome with no real personality. I guessed that's why I wasn't attracted to him.

"I was coming to tell you to have a good weekend," he said.

Smiling, I said, "You too." When I didn't elaborate, he waved, and let himself out of my office.

Shaking my head, I suppose I should be happy that men were after me. It would make my mother happy to know her daughter was out here causing men to beat down my door. After Amir, she was more disappointed than I was.

It's like the older I became, the less she had hope that I'd pop her out some grandbabies. She was too traditional to want me procreating children out of wedlock, so that made her nerves even worse. While I didn't live my life solely to please my parents, I didn't want to disappoint them either. The pressure was real, though, to at least have a husband and children one day.

Sighing, I touched the spot where Grim's lips had met my skin, and my lips.

Just three more weeks, Mila.

CHAPTER 2

SPADE 'GRIM' GRAHAM

"Nothin' in you feels sorry for what you doin', bruh?"

Peering across the table at the nigga wasting my damn time, I dragged from my blunt and regarded his question.

"Sure, I do," I answered truthfully.

He shook his head indignantly. "You'on feel shit," he replied.

"But I do," I disagreed. "I feel some typa way that ya family gon' suffer from ya greed. What's more fucked up; yeen feel no typa way for bringin' this on ya family."

While he chuckled, I exhaled another round of smoke.

"Choose which one I'm takin'," I ordered.

He leaned forward and rested his arms on the table separating us, prompting my cousin, Choppa, to do the same.

"Watch what you doin'," Choppa warned.

"Mane, ain't nobody on that dumb shit. Like Grim said, I got a family." His sarcasm did nothing but make me smirk.

"Answer my question. This is my last time askin'," I said.

He chuckled. "Askin'? You really think-"

"*I think* you betta answer my question, Irv."

"You makin' me choose between my life and how I feed my family." He grabbed his head and dug his fingers into his locks. "Hand me the fuckin' papers."

"Sign everywhere I've placed an 'x'," my lawyer, Keisha, told him.

Irv grilled her.

"Careful how you lookin' at my wife," Choppa drawled.

Irv snatched the papers up, then angrily begin signing them. I ashed my blunt and waited for him to finish. Once he was done, he shoved the papers back toward Keisha, who collected them with a gracious smile.

"Glad we could do business," I stated.

"Fuck you!" Irv spat as Choppa made him stand.

"You shouldn't be angry with me. Be angry with yaself for tryna come for me. You better be glad I'm in a good mood, and you're walkin' away with ya life. You can start another business and provide for ya family. The alternative..."

Irv flipped me the bird causing me to grit my back teeth but shrug. With a nod of my head, Choppa led Irv out of the conference room with Keisha following.

My cell vibrated just as I stood from the table.

My Love: We hope your night is going well! So proud of you! Love you!

I read my mother's message with a smile as I exited the conference room. Without having to tell them, two of my security guards followed me as I made my way down the hall, down the stairs, and to the first floor of my club.

Me: Everything is perfect, ma. Love y'all too!

Head in my phone, I kept it moving all the way to the bar. Kaleef, my bar manager, placed a drink in front of me as I approached.

"Grim? You got a minute?"

I glanced behind me at the brunette sista requesting my time. Sharika was bad and looked exceptionally fuckable tonight in the black cocktail dress she wore. Her long legs were made for being stretched wide, and I had a time or two.

"What is it?" I asked, not really trying to entertain her. Beautiful as she was, Sharika was a shark. If I gave her a minute too long, she'd be in this bitch pretending like she and I were a couple.

"It's loud in here," she said over the music. As if that was supposed to make me take her somewhere quieter.

"It's a club, shawty. Kaleef can hear in five o'clock Atlanta traffic, from a mile away, though." Kaleef chucked his head at her, confirming what the fuck I said.

Tonight, was the grand opening of my newest club The Code II. Aside from dealing with Irv, things had gone well so far. I had several guests in the building, all of whom I welcomed to enjoy themselves. People were still filing in, none of which had my attention more than the beauty strutting through the entrance with her friends.

I bit my lip to stifle the growl on my lips at the piece of scrap she had on showing off what would soon belong to me. Mila had a body that, in one word, was exquisite. That shit was tall, supple, and curvy as fuck. She strutted her ass around like her body wasn't the shit.

But her face—that's what drew me like a king to his queen. Mila's perfect sun kissed brown face was made for me to gaze at nonstop. Her deep, expressive brown eyes, perfectly full arched eyebrows, high ass cheekbones, and cute nose fit perfectly in her oval-shaped face.

Two years—that's how long it'd been since I first laid eyes on her. Damn if I knew I was at a wedding though. My eyes stayed on Mila the entire service. After the nuptials were exchanged, I sought Mila out, only to find her booed up with a nigga that looked like he was uncomfortable as fuck in his surroundings. Not deterred by her nigga, I couldn't resist approaching Mila and letting her know how muthafuckin' sexy she was. She was shocked by my boldness. Her nigga, however, mugged me.

Thankfully, for him, I was in a good mood that day.

I left the church after my cousin Darren called himself saving ol' boy.

Just because she was taken didn't keep me from asking about her whenever I talked to my cousin. He played shit off, not really trying to entertain my questions when it came to his wife's best friend.

After sitting through the first class with her being my professor, I called Darren to see what was up with shawty. He reluctantly told me that she and her dude had split due to him cheating on her. I wasn't surprised at all to know that her ex was just as fucking dumb as he looked.

There I was, poised to take his woman and didn't.

Damn. Fate had a funny way of bringing things, and people, back into alignment. Because I swear, Mila was that classy ass, boss bitch that a nigga like me wouldn't have any problems bowing to.

Overhearing her conversation yesterday, I knew she'd be here tonight and had reserved a VIP for her and her friends. That way I could keep my eyes on her and make sure none of these dusty ass niggas got within reach of her.

I waded through the crowd towards Mila, or as I preferred to call her, my professor. As immature as it seemed, I enjoyed toying with her in class. She did her best to ignore the fuck out of me, but I wouldn't let her. Every chance I was presented, I made sure she knew that I was coming for her ass. The past couple of months had been nothing short of torture sitting in that damn lecture hall feasting on her presence, yet knowing I wasn't taking her home with me.

But shit was about to change. I had enough of her playing like she didn't want me, which is how I ended up in her office yesterday. She needed to be honest and quit playing games with me. I caught her subtle glances during class when she thought I wasn't looking. And I definitely peeped the way her body responded to me whenever I was close to her.

I wasn't the man to chase any female. However, I was in hot pursuit of Mila. From that moment two years ago, I knew I'd one day have her.

"This club is nice!" I heard Lucy say as I approached. They had their backs to me as they surveyed the club.

The Code II was a business venture I took up after opening my first club The Code I in Destin, Florida which was a little over an hour away. At the time I had just turned twenty-eight and was looking for a way to capitalize off the money I'd made in the dope game.

The success of my clubs coupled with other real estate I owned made me a wealthy man.

All I was missing was my degree. It's the one thing my parents wanted that I hadn't given them yet. So, here I was at thirty-two, months away from being a college graduate.

"Good evenin', ladies," I spoke sidling up behind Mila.

She whirled around with her eyes wide as saucers as she took me in.

"Mr. Graham!" Mila's breathless, caramel smooth voice caused the same reaction in me that it always did.

"We're not in class, *Mila*," I responded. "How're you doin' tonight?" Judging by the black bandage dress she had on with all those fucking cut outs in it, and the stilettoes on her pretty ass feet, I'd say shawty was trying to get someone's attention. I'ain like that.

She smoothed her hand down her sleek black, bone straight hair that reached her shoulders and nervously chuckled. *That*, I did like.

"Good evenin'," I spoke to Kai and Lucy. As always, the two were beautiful. However, they were just as naked as Mila.

"D and Chuck know y'all outchea dressed like that?" I questioned. They both mumbled under their breaths which meant no. "I'ain no snitch, but y'all chill out tonight. I'on want no smoke." Their husbands were just as deadly as I was.

"Uhm...Spade-"

"Grim," I corrected Mila. She was gon' say my shit one day.

"*Spade*," she acknowledged instead.

Smiling, I said, "Why don't I get y'all a seat in VIP and get you some drinks goin'."

She shook her head 'no' while Kai and Lucy opposed her.

"We can't ask you to do that. We can get our own section," Mila informed me.

"That's not necessary. I already have a section prepared for you, love," I smoothly informed her.

Her mouth opened and closed. "What? How?" Her eyes narrowed on me. "You were listening to my phone call?"

"Actually, you were on speaker, so it was kinda difficult *not* to listen." The expression on her face caused me to laugh. "Besides, Lucy is my cousin-in-law. Y'all never have to pay for shit when y'all come to anything I own."

Mila rolled her eyes.

"Thank you, Grim," Lucy said.

"So, can I treat y'all?" My question was directed at Mila, but Kai and Lucy answered.

Mila acquiesced, not wanting to put a damper on their night.

As I led them to VIP, I placed my hand at the small of Mila's back. She flinched from the contact, bringing a smile to my face. The little gesture caused a rise in my blood pressure too.

Once we made it to the section, I had one of the bottle girls bring them whatever they requested. Reluctantly, Mila thanked me.

"This was unnecessary, though," she said.

"Not to me. I want you ladies to enjoy your night. Y'all need anything, I'll be close by." As much as I wanted to stay in this section and be up under Mila, I had to tend to business. If this wasn't my grand opening, I would've been by her side. However, people expected to see my face and socialize with me.

The luxury of my VIP sections was that security kept anyone out who wasn't a part of any party paying for a section. Figuring I could handle work and oversee Mila's section, I stepped away from the section only to stand by the railing overlooking the club's open floor.

Glancing over my shoulder, I caught Mila staring. I winked at her just to fuck with her. Yeah, I was going to stay my ass right here and conduct whatever business I had to from this spot. Mila was looking too good for me to let her out of my eyesight.

*****

The night flowed well, with me meeting prospective associates. Everyone wanted a piece of the mind that was Grim. Many niggas were outchea making money, but not like me. Those who sought insight on going legit approached me, wondering how I was able to do it. I helped those who really sought freedom and brushed off those who clearly were the ops.

Besides dealing with business, I did have to rebuff the advances of several women. They were blocking like a muthafucka. Every time a female approached me, I checked to see Mila's reaction. It comforted me to find her watching me, stale faced. To me, that was comforting.

Now that my guests were settled and enjoying themselves, and the ladies finally let me be, I got back to stalking Mila. I hadn't left my spot outside of her section, casually glancing back every now and then to see if she was good.

She, Kai, and Lucy partied as if I wasn't standing here, and as if Kai and Lucy didn't have husbands to go home to. They had all eyes on them, and I couldn't even be mad. Women who commanded attention without being overtly sexual were enigmas to me.

Admittedly, the allure of such a female intimidated me—and I wasn't intimidated by anything. Mila held that type of pull over me. I could hardly focus on anyone who'd approached me tonight for watching her gyrate to the music thumping through the speakers. Every time the DJ dropped a new joint, she relaxed even more.

"Can I get you something to drink, boss?"

Dapping my little brother, Kain, I shook my head. "I'm good tonight."

He chuckled and flicked his eyes toward Mila. "You're determined to have shawty." So obvious

Mila just so happened to step out of the section, glancing around for something.

"What do you need, baby?" I asked her.

She snapped her eyes at me. "Restroom," she said over the shouts of the crowd as the DJ spun another banger.

"I'll take you," I offered, causing Kain to chuckle. The three followed me through the club until we were walking up a set of stairs, down the hallway, and into my office. I invited them in and left them to it while I stood outside my office door.

"Keepin' a close eye on her," my head of security, Nick, commented. His job was to make sure no one came up the stairs leading to my office and to handle any business pertaining to shit breaking off in the club. His keen observation is what garnered him his position.

"And?"

Nick chuckled. "*And*, I see why, my dawg." He dapped me as he passed me to stroll the hallway.

Ten minutes later, a loud burst of laughter sounded from inside my office just as the door opened. Mila bumped right into my chest.

"Oh, damn!" she exclaimed when she almost busted her ass. I was swift, though, and caught her from falling.

"Did you purposely do that?" she fussed as she smoothed her dress down.

"Nah," I answered, trying not to drool over her bare thighs.

"We apologize for Mila's behavior," Kai said. "We're trying to get her to loosen up some."

I stared down at Mila and licked my lips just because I was itching to taste hers. She wore a nude color on her bow shaped, juicy lips. On the inside, I grinned at the way she stopped breathing from me standing too close.

"You need to loosen up, Mila?" I questioned. "I can help you with that."

She ignored the sounds Kai and Lucy made while eyeing me. "I already told you we can't-"

"We can," I smoothly interjected. Finally, we were about to have this talk.

"No, we can't. You're trying to make me lose everything I've worked hard for," she emphasized. "Fucking with a student is grounds for termination."

"I wouldn't dare cause you to lose anything. If anything, I want you to have it all."

We were standing so close that her perfume made love to my senses.

"Just so you can fuck me?" she questioned; eyebrows drawn together.

Tilting my head to the side, I bit down into my bottom lip. Kai's and Lucy's sharp intake of breath said that they were shocked by their friend's boldness.

"Who says I wanna fuck you, lil' baby?"

She swallowed and narrowed her eyes at me.

"Says the many sexual comments you've made toward me. If this isn't about fucking, then what is it about?" she queried.

"Mila!" Lucy hissed, but Kai shushed her. They were all in the business like this was their fantasy. I'd give the three of them something to ponder on.

"It's about me feastin' on every part of you until we're both weak. It's about me watchin' the play of emotions on ya face while I...do those unspeakable things to you. Remember we talked about that, right?" I teased.

"Sounds like fucking," she breathlessly stated.

Leaning down until we were eye level with each other, I said, "Sounds like raw passion, soaked sheets, strained voices, *multiple* orgasms, late night soaks, and good ass fuckin' sleep afterwards."

Kai and Lucy made another incomprehensible noise.

"Ya birthday is comin'. Allow me to make it a memorable one." This was the perfect opportunity to show Mila that I was serious.

She contemplated it, only for a second. "I can't," she said again. "If we get caught-"

"We can leave town," I rebutted. Everything she threw at me I tossed back the solution.

"Mr.-"

I gave her a look.

"*Spade*," she groaned cutely.

"Tell me no, and I'll leave you alone," I said, then wished I hadn't. If she told me no, then pursuing her afterwards would be weird as fuck. Thus far, she'd never uttered anything to make me stay away from her. She was too busy making excuses for why we couldn't have each other.

"Like I said," she continued. "We can't."

Her friends smacked their teeth, disappointed by Mila turning me down.

Still, she hadn't voiced 'no' causing me to chuckle.

"Aight, baby," I relented. For now.

I could tell she hated she had to decline my offer by the way she studied me as I led them back to their VIP section. Like I'd done the whole night, I stood outside the section making sure they were straight and keeping these thirsty ass niggas away from my woman.

CHAPTER 3

MILA

"I've never been the one to force you to do something, but bitch, this is the time that I will," Lucy stated. "You got that giant, sexy ass nigga chasing after you and all you're worried about is work!"

I cut my eyes at Lucy, who sat across the booth from me. We were out having lunch until their men made it home from work. Work being the warehouse where both of their husbands did unmentionables by day and night.

"Should I tell Darren you're around here referring to his cousin as 'giant' and 'sexy ass'? And this work *that you speak of is how I pay my bills. Not only that but it's my reputation on the line."*

"You're deflecting by bringing Darren in this," Kai instigated. "Grim said himself that y'all could leave town.

This man is literally doing whatever he can just to have you, Mila. If you lie and say you don't want Grim, I'm going to assume you're ready to branch out and try women."

I smacked my teeth. "Kai, I've tried women before, remember?" It was fleeting, but still.

"Tried for one week with one female. That doesn't count," Lucy said.

"Exactly," Kai added. "Just admit that you want him and go for what he's giving."

Sighing, I looked at my two best friends and shook my head.

"Y'all could be advocating for a serial killer. How would y'all feel if I ended up dead messing around with him? This is the man who has Grim as a street name."

Kai pecked away at her phone while Lucy pursed her lips.

"Grim is harmless, Mila."

"Tuh!" I rebutted. "Any man that confidently approaches a woman while she's with her man, and all but says he wants to take you home, is not wrapped too tight. Mind you, Amir wasn't some punk back then."

They both cracked up.

"That's forever going down in history!" Lucy laughed. "The look on your face had Amir stuck."

Shaking my head, I replied, "That's probably why his ass cheated on me."

Kai scoffed. "No, the hell it isn't! He cheated long after that and because he wanted to."

Lucy agreed. "Any man that doesn't take the time to celebrate and appreciate his woman is up to something no good. He's never even bought you a gift for any occasion. That right there is just ridiculous. Then for his ass to have the nerve to try to win you back after he trampled all over your feelings is psycho."

I hated reliving my nightmare of a relationship with Amir.

"Facts," Kai seconded. "But back to Grim. So, what if he's a little-"

"Crazy," I supplied. They snickered.

"Rough around the edges," Kai finished. "Darren and Chuck have nothing bad to say about him."

Shaking my head, I replied, "Darren and Chuck aren't good examples, boo. They're crazy too."

They busted out laughing.

"Seriously, Mila, Grim is low-key. He stays out of the way and minds his business."

I rolled my eyes. "Please stop trying to make him look like an angel. Did you see the way those women were tripping over themselves last night?"

"Did you see the way he politely dismissed them?" Lucy questioned.

Smacking my teeth, I asked, "Why are y'all so intent on me fucking with him?"

They both looked at me like I was stupid.

"'Cause, he has I will fuck you up *written all over him, and that's exactly what you need to get you out of this slump you're in," Lucy offered.*

"Let the church say, amen," Kai mumbled before sipping her tea.

Monday afternoon was like a ghost waiting for me in a darkened closet. As I reflected on the conversation I'd had with Kai and Lucy, I was worked up like hell. Knowing I'd have to face Spade today set my body ablaze. The shit he'd said to me Friday night was still fresh in my mind and had me using my rose three nights in a row.

What's worse, the way Spade looked Friday night didn't compare to the way he looked while in class. The black denim jeans and black Polo shirt he'd worn melded to his thick body like a tight coochie to a big dick. It was a horrible analysis, but that's all I could think of when I laid eyes on him that night. He looked like straight back-to-back orgasms.

Then he had the nerve to have a grill in his mouth. It sat on his lower teeth, turning his already sexy, arrogant demeanor into a savage one. If he oozed sex before, I couldn't even describe what he'd oozed then. Lastly, the ice he wore...it literally lit him up.

Lord, I wasn't sure how I was going to get through this class, but I had to get my shit together. As students started filing in, behind my desk, my leg shook nervously. Amongst the students, a guy in a uniform walked in carrying a vase of roses.

"Hello," he spoke. "Ms. Dash?"

I nodded. He sat the roses on my desk and left with a wave.

Turning my nose up at the roses, I knew damn well Amari hadn't popped up sending me shit. My birthday was this Saturday, but he'd never gotten me a damn thing for the occasion. Besides, I hadn't heard from him since I left Mobile.

"Don't tell me this nigga is about to start this bullshit," I mumbled to myself.

The card attached to the flowers ended up in my hand. Although I wanted to burn it, I opened it to see what his fool ass had to say.

My professor,

297 Tall Pines Loop, Destin.

-Grim

"Nice roses."

I jumped out of my skin at the sound of Spade's voice. His smirk was everything as he sauntered to the section of the lecture hall he preferred. When he cocked his legs open and got comfortable, only then did I realize I was staring.

Stuffing the card in my pocket, I pulled my head out of the clouds and proceeded to teach my class as best as I could under the circumstances. The circumstances being—I wanted Spade Graham in the worst way.

It was hell getting through my lecture between the smell of the roses and the presence of Spade. Once class ended, I exhaled a deep breath of relief.

"See you Wednesday, my professor," Spade said as he passed my desk.

I shot daggers at his back, wishing he'd somehow miss my class on Wednesday.

*****

Suspiciously, I stared at the roses the same delivery man from yesterday placed on my desk. First, why the hell was he delivering them to my lecture hall instead of my office? It was like Spade wanted this show just so he could see my reaction.

Speaking of Spade, he wasn't in class yet, so hopefully my wish came true. Kai cussed me out last night after I told her about the card and roses. She all but threatened to kill me if I didn't find my ass at his house this weekend.

"Another set of roses?" One of my female students commented with a smile. I nodded and nervously smiled.

Reluctantly, I took the small envelope out, which was slightly puffy. I opened the envelope to a card...and a key with the bow shaped as the letter M with what looked like real diamonds embedded in it.

My professor,

Unlock what I have to offer, baby. Although I crave ya sexy ass body, I crave ya sexy ass mind even more. Let me tap into it.

-Grim

"Damn, somebody's on that ass heavy."

Again, I nearly had a heart attack at the sound of Spade's deep drawl.

"Yeen lyin'." Another one of my male students was walking by and decided to add his two cents.

Spade eyed him, then chuckled. "I'on blame him, though. I'm sure he'on mind bodyin' a nigga 'bout her either."

My eyes stretched to the heavens at Spade's comment. Orlando, the other student, laughed like he didn't see a problem with what Spade said.

"Shiidd, which is why I keep my distance," Orlando replied.

What the hell?

Spade laughed. "Yeah, you betta do that, big dawg."

"Gentlemen!" I hissed. "Take your seats, please."

While Orlando did as I said, Spade lingered back.

"I like that bossy shit," he quipped for my ears only.

I choked on nothing and tapped my chest to keep my heart from popping out of it. What churned my nerves was the way he laughed as he sauntered to his seat.

I fumbled through class and broke my neck trying to make my escape by the time it was over.

That night I showered and settled on my sofa with a bowl of salad and a glass of wine. I really needed a strong drink to knock Spade off my mind, but I had one more day of classes to get through before my weekend started.

As I flipped through channels, my phone chimed with a message.

The number wasn't one I recognized.

Wish I could celebrate your birthday with you. I miss you. Amir.

My eyes bugged, and the message promptly spoiled my appetite. Sitting the salad aside, I damn near wanted to throw up while hurrying to get the message out of my phone.

"I think the hell not!" I quickly blocked the number, then deleted the message. My number was one I hadn't changed after leaving Mobile. Once I'd blocked him, he never tried to reach out to me, so I assumed I was in the clear.

Poised to call Lucy and Kai, a message came through from Lucy.

Lucy: You better do it!

Kai: Or we're going to unfriend you, sis.

I groaned.

Me: Just had to block a number! Amir texted me!

Kai: IKYFL!!!!

Lucy: IKYFL!

Instead of texting back a response, I called Lucy, then added Kai to the call.

"My weekend is already ruined, and it hasn't started." I pinched the bridge of my nose, totally stressed after receiving that message.

"No ma'am!" Kai fussed. "What you not gon' do is allow Amir to drag his filthy ass back into your mind, let alone your life. You have plans this weekend and not one person is disrupting that!"

My head snapped back.

"What plans do I have, Kai?"

"Lord," Lucy mumbled. "You have plans with Grim, Mila."

"No-"

"Aht, aht!" Kai barked. "*You have plans with Grim!*"

"But-"

"No excuses," Lucy shot. "We're not accepting any from you."

Sighing, my eyes fell on the key sitting atop my coffee table. It stared back at me, enchanting me. It was a beautiful key, and I know if used, would open a door to many nights of pleasure. Pleasure wasn't the problem, though. It was trouble—trouble with two, maybe three, thick long legs, a thick beard, hard chest, and a sexy as sin smile.

"If something happens to me, I'm blaming y'alls trifling asses. Won't y'all go make some babies or something and get out of my business," I joked. Neither Kai nor Lucy was in a hurry to have children.

Although...

"Wait a damn minute!" I shrieked. "Kai! Lucy!"

They both grumbled.

"In my defense, I just found out for sure this morning," Kai said. "I was going to tell you after the weekend was over."

Lucy smacked her teeth. "I told you not having at least one drink would make her suspicious."

Recalling the night we were at the club, Kai and Lucy nursed the same drink the entire night, neither or which they drank. While I put three away, I was too busy dancing and enjoying myself to notice that my friends hadn't had the first sip of their drinks.

"I should kick y'alls asses," I grumbled.

They snickered.

"We wanted to wait until after your birthday," Lucy stated.

"So, is this why y'all are so intent on me giving up my virginity to Grim?"

They fell out laughing.

Grinning, I shook my head at them. "If I lose my job behind this, one of y'all gotta take me in, and the other one has to pay for my therapy after my parents disown me."

Because who was I kidding? I was about to jump off a cliff for a man I barely knew just because he intrigued me and turned me on to no end. Could I lose my job? Definitely. Did I care. Hell yes! But the purring between my legs, and my girls on the other end of the phone wouldn't let me resist Spade.

Again, my eyes met the diamond encrusted key. Spade probably had a treasure trove of keys he doled out to women. Yet, I *still* wasn't turned off by his advances.

"Bet," they both responded at the same time.

Rolling my eyes, I hung up, and placed my phone down while remembering the smell of Spade. First, I smelled the marijuana, then the Chanel he wore. I couldn't get the mixture out of my head.

What are you doing, Mila?

RMU was a big school, but in this city, everyone knew each other. Spade wasn't just a student, he had status outside of the university. If anything got back to Mrs. Jackie, it would devastate her and my parents.

Yet, something about Spade willed me to go against everything I believed in, scaring me. Forbidden fruit came in the form of Spade Graham. Taking a bite out of him could end me.

*****

Thursday afternoon...

As soon as class was over, I power walked to my office and handled the little business waiting for me. Two hours later, I was in my car headed to Destin, key resting in the passenger seat, riding shotgun. I packed enough to tide me over for a few days.

The purpose of me popping up on Spade was to throw him off his game. Spade was always so calm and cool as if nothing rattled him. As arrogant as he was, he expected me to show up to his house, just not a day early. If things went okay this evening, then I'd let things naturally progress.

I prayed I wasn't making the biggest mistake of my life.

GRIM

The flashing of my security alarm signaled that someone was at the gate. Smiling, I deactivated the alarm and allowed the gate to open. As Mila's black Acura crept up the circular driveway, I finished my last set of arm curls then placed the weight to the side.

"You got company?"

On the television, I watched Mila park behind my Cadillac but not get out of her car. Although a day early, I had no doubt that she would show. She was mine and she knew it. My soul called to hers, drawing her to me whether she liked it or not.

Only she *did* like it. If it was not for her being my professor, Mila and I would be well on our way to an engagement by now. However, because of university policy, Mila could lose everything by fucking with me.

Me wanting her regardless of what the repercussions were could be construed as selfish. However, I wasn't selfish in the least. I had big plans for Mila, plans that went beyond a fucking policy book.

"Yo', is that who I think it is?"

"Damn, shole is."

Those were my brothers Jacari and Tito. The two of them, along with Kain, were at my house working out with me as they normally did a few days a week. Although younger than me, Kain and Jacari were married while Tito was engaged to be married this summer.

Kain chuckled as we watched Mila pace the area next to her car.

Kain, being the oldest under me knew of my feelings for Mila. Jacari and Tito heard me talk about her every now and then, but they did not realize the depth of my need for Mila.

"Y'all niggas gotta bounce," I informed them, earning me some grumbles. While they gathered their shit, I marveled at Mila's frame as she contemplated her next move. When she glided toward the house, I left out of my home gym, and decided to wait by the front door to see if she would be bold enough to use the key I had given her.

It took her a whole five minutes to get up the nerve to insert the key. She slowly opened the door, her eyes wide as she glanced around the sun lit foyer before they fell on me. Her brown orbs grew even wider.

"You're naked," she whispered, and went to close the door while she stayed outside.

Chuckling, I bounded to the door and snatched it open. She stood there with the key still clutched in her hand, staring at the door. When she realized my chest was in front of her, she unhurriedly tracked her gaze up my body.

"Careful now," I warned. "I'm not naked by the way."

She gulped as our eyes connected.

"I mean…you…" she stuttered. "You have on nothing but shorts."

Reaching my hand out, I grabbed hers, then brought her inside, closing the door behind her. Pushing her straight strands behind her ears, I cupped both sides of her face and brought her lips to mine, gently pecking them, surprising her. Our eyes never closed but held each other's.

"Just finished workin' out," I informed her. As she gathered her thoughts, I kissed her cheeks, then wrapped my arms around her for a tight hug. She softened against me, then put her arms around my back. When her hands touched my bare back, I had to fight to keep my dick from reacting. We had to treat our guest with respect, and him showing out this quickly would run her off. Lol

"Without your heels you're short as hell, baby," I commented with a grin. I loved the way her head rested against my chest, though.

"You're just really tall," she said.

"Aight, bruh, we'll catch up witcha," Tito said as he, Kain, and Jacari met us in the foyer.

Mila's body stiffened in my arms.

"'Sup, lil' baby?" Kain spoke, followed by Jacari and Tito.

"Hi," she croaked out. Nervously, she glanced back and forth between them.

"These are my brothers." I introduced them by name.

"Right..." She tried to pull away from me, but I pulled her closer.

"You're straight, shawty, no worries," I assured her. No one was supposed to know she was here and seeing my brothers made her anxious.

"All is well," Jacari seconded as they filed out of the house, closing the door behind them.

"You're early," I quipped.

"Oh, I can leave," she shot back. "I already feel like I'm worth a couple dollars from traipsing my ass over here *and* being surprised to see people here besides you."

Laughing, I hugged her tighter. She squealed as I lifted her off her feet, threw her over my shoulder, and carried her through my room and into the bathroom.

I deposited Mila on the edge of the tub, which was next to the walk-in shower that could easily fit an entire family.

"Don't ever refer to yaself as a hooker. I only said that 'cause had I known you were on the way I would've sent them home before you got here. Otherwise, we're two adults that find each other highly attractive and decided to act on that shit. I've been watchin' you for months, and I can tell no nigga's been between those thighs."

She gasped. "What-"

"Your walk has never changed," I said by way of explanation.

She scoffed.

"Besides, yeen goin' anywhere without me." We faced off with me daring her to move.

"I'm not about to watch you shower," she stated, changing the subject.

Smirking, I strode inside the shower and cut it on. "Why not? I don't mind. You can even join me," I offered.

Rolling her eyes away from me, she focused on the floor while I undressed.

"Shit..." she mumbled.

"What's that?"

Mila's mouth was ajar as a deep stain marred her cheeks. She quickly averted her gaze away from my dick.

Chuckling, I stepped under the shower's spray and fought the urge to snatch her up while I cleaned my body. She'd steal a glance here and there, but for the most part kept her eyes on the floor.

I made quick work of cleaning my body, drying off, and shucking another pair of shorts on.

"So, you're just going to walk around half-naked?" she questioned.

Hunching my shoulder, I said, "It's just you and me in here, and we're on the beach. Matter fact, you got too many clothes on." I winked at her then beckoned her to follow me out of the bathroom.

"You brought luggage?"

She nodded as she observed my bedroom. It was surrounded on two sides by glass and overlooking the balcony and semi-private beach. I considered it semi-private because muhfuckas still straggled down this way every now and then.

My neighbors were as secluded as I was, so I never worried about them wondering what I had going on over here.

"Can people see inside here?" She walked over to place her hand on the thick glass as she beheld the waves rumbling and crashing just a walk away.

Sidling up behind her, I brought my body flush with hers. Although her breath quickened, she didn't flinch. I eased my hands into my pockets and shook my head.

"Not unless I allow them to." I leaned in and gently kissed her neck enjoying how the hair her skin rose. "If you want, we can allow viewers."

She glanced at me over her shoulder with her eyebrows pinched together.

"I'd have to kill 'em afterwards, though. After me, no one's gon' see you ass naked and not see me."

Chuckling, she turned back to the view. "You sound deranged, Spade. We're only together for the weekend."

CHAPTER 4

MILA

Spade's chuckle drew my nipples into pebbles. Deranged is exactly how he sounded. His deep voice coupled with his dick against my ass had me overheating in my biker short set. He claimed I was over-dressed, while I felt butt naked. The smell of his fresh skin toyed with my nostrils causing them to flare.

"I don't like to share," he said.

"But, after the weekend is over, that won't be your issue," I uttered. I couldn't read between the lines of the smile on his face, so I figured we had an understanding.

"How about you get comfortable while I get your things out of the car," he suggested.

We left his neatly kept bedroom with the big ass bed situated against the wall. The neatly carved headboard was so elaborate that I stared.

Back in the living room, I beheld the beauty of Spade's house. I was accustomed to nice things, but his house was exquisite—mainly the crisp gray furnishings and sparkling chandeliers.

While I plopped down on the plush sofa, Spade ambled towards the front door.

Sighing, I let my gaze roam his living room again. Pictures of his family dominated the same wall as the fireplace. The large flat screen television mounted to the wall was on, but muted.

Doing as Spade said, I kicked my slides off and reached for the remote, which was on the glass coffee table, and cut the volume up.

He came back into the house minutes later carrying my pink duffle bag and my purse. His barefoot ass was so damn fine. His magnificently built chest seemed to be carved with the sharpest blade. His tattoos seemed to be chaotic as there were so many that I couldn't decipher one from the other.

"You like to stare, huh?" he joked as he passed me and went to the bedroom. I gulped because he was putting my things in his room as if the statement he'd made about me not going anywhere was true.

He appeared again with his phone to his ear. "You want to eat out or in, baby girl?" he asked although I'm sure he knew the answer.

"In." Even an hour away from home, I couldn't be too careful.

"Yeah, come through," he said to whoever was on the other end of his phone before hanging up.

My eyes bucked.

He laughed. "Chill, shawty. Yeen gotta worry about anybody comin' through here on some bullshit. I got you," he assured. "We're gon' enjoy each other and fuck everything else."

Standing over me, he took my hand and brought me to my feet.

"The sun is going down, and the chef will be here any minute to make us dinner. Why don't you go change into something more comfortable," he proposed.

"This is comfortable," I replied.

"I mean...a lil' more comfortable," he clarified with a flick of his tongue across his thick lips. "Make yaself completely at home."

I found myself in his bedroom, rifling through my bag for a pair of boy shorts. If I was at home, I dressed in boy shorts and a sports bra. Because Spade had my panties a little damp already, I thought it best to freshen up before I changed.

Forty-five minutes later, I emerged from the room to the sounds of slow jams, low lighting, lit candles, and the smell of food being slayed. A large, thick pallet covered the living room floor. On top of it were plush body pillows, and two more blankets. From where I stood, the view of the ocean to my left brought a smile to my face.

Spade's place was absolutely stunning. Now that the sun had set, the moon and sprinkling of stars cast a beautiful glow over the water calling anyone within eyesight to take notice of its beauty.

Spade was in the kitchen speaking with another gentlemen. They were laughing loud as hell. My ears perked up to see if they were talking about me in my absence. I relaxed upon hearing them mentioning pro basketball.

"I'm glad you decided to make yaself at home."

Spade startled me.

"Why do you keep sneaking up on me?" Turning, I found Spade sauntering my way holding two flutes, a bottle of champagne, and a corkscrew.

He chortled. "I don't. Ya head is just always somewhere else." He bit into his bottom lip while his eyes fell to my belly button.

"Am I too underdressed?" He continued to stare, so I had to ask.

"You're perfect." He motioned to the pallet. "The food will be done shortly. Allow me to get to know Mila, and I'd love for you to get to know me."

Mila never sounded so good coming off someone's lips as it did coming off Spade's. It's like he made my whole being melt whenever he uttered my name.

"Sure," I agreed.

I hadn't been on a traditional picnic in some time, but this living room picnic set up had me in love. The minute I crawled under one of the blankets, a sense of peace and lightness filled me, which was strange considering I barely knew Spade. However, whatever peace overtook me had me relaxing enough to recline against the sofa.

I was here now, and from the first kiss Spade had me stuck. That sweet little peck he placed on me was unexpected yet endearing. My plan to surprise him and throw him off his game turned into me wondering what it would be like to have a man do sweet things like this occasionally.

Kai and Lucy always ragged me about not having a man but deep down, I was better off without one. After escaping the bullshit with Amir, I didn't want anything that resembled the toxic shit I went through with him.

This weekend with Spade would scratch an itch so to speak. Then I could go back to my normal, boring life.

Spade joined me on the pallet, bringing me out of my thoughts. He sat right up under me causing me to smile. After popping the champagne, he filled a flute, then handed it to me. He did the same for himself. He held his flute out so we could toast.

"To new beginnings," he stated.

Tilting my head to the side, I parroted, "New beginnings." Our flutes clanked with our gazes locked. Why did it feel like I'd just signed up for something without reading the fine print? Spade's grin didn't offer me any reassurance. He sat his drink aside and produced a blunt out of thin air, then sparked up. The smell was potent, but I didn't complain as he casually dragged from it.

He positioned my legs across his and his arm over my shoulder, bringing me closer.

"Tell me what made you want to become an educator."

He laughed when I sighed.

"Both of my parents are educators," I answered. "I wanted nothing to do with teaching, but I somehow fell in love with it my first year in. It's been five years now, and I couldn't imagine doing anything else."

He chuckled. "I was shocked as hell when I walked in class and saw you standin' there. I thought I was dreamin'. You know you dominate my dreams, right?"

Flattered, I smiled. "No comment," I replied.

Moving on, he asked, "Siblings?"

I shook my head. "Kai and Lucy are my best friends, but we act like sisters. Any other siblings besides your brothers?"

He smirked. "My mom wanted another baby but feared she'd have another boy, so she gave it up."

Chuckling, I said, "I don't blame her. You and your brothers seem like y'all cause all types of hell."

He playfully scoffed. "I'm an angel."

I threw my head back and laughed. "No, the hell you're not! You're the same man that threatened another one of my students."

Shrugging, he replied, "I'on like to share."

"So, you've said." I sipped my champagne and studied him. Spade made no effort to deny that he'd threatened someone in the manner he had. If I really believed what was in his eyes, I'd see a man that most likely lived up to what he'd said. Clearing my throat, I glanced away and downed the rest of my champagne.

"I mean it too," he added. That only made me gulp.

"You seem to be doing great for yourself. Why are you single?" I assumed he was single. For all I knew, Spade probably had a harem of women.

What does that say for you being half-naked in his house?

"I'm single 'cause my professor is single."

"That makes no sense," I stated as he offered me more champagne. I declined for the moment. Whatever the chef was cooking had my stomach rumbling to try it. I'd have a glass once dinner was served.

"It makes perfect sense," he replied after ashing his blunt. He then brought his drink to his lips and sipped it. "Until you allow me to be ya man, I'm single."

My man?

He grinned from the expression written across my face.

"I shouldn't even be here, Spade," I reminded him.

"But you are. Anything's possible."

Why did I feel like this man was even crazier than my ex? The look in Spade's eyes as he studied me over the rim of his glass sent chills down my spine. It occurred to me, yet again, that I was risking my entire livelihood for a weekend with Spade.

How crazy.

*****

We continued talking even after Spade placed our plates on the pallet. I appreciated him for not allowing the chef to see me.

Over dessert, I listened to Spade break down his family's dynamics. I loved how he spoke so highly of his brothers. His older brother instinct was clear as he mentioned how he didn't play when it came to them. So it was with his parents; his love ran deep for his family.

I learned two of his brothers were married, and one was set to be married soon. When he mentioned that his brothers were on his case about settling down, I resisted the urge to smile from ear to ear. What caught my attention is that he didn't speak against settling down. Admittedly, that made me curious.

Spade was so easy to listen and talk to that I opened up about my family. My parents loved me to no end and vice versa. I explained how Kai, Lucy, and I became friends which had him in stitches.

"I can only imagine the shit y'all got into," he said.

"Plenty," I answered with a smile.

He smiled in return and peered at me with a million other questions dancing in his eyes.

"It's no wonder I'm in love with you."

In love?

There was one thing for a man to feel a particular way about a woman. However, for him to actually express it to her was an entirely different ball game.

Laughing it off, I said, "There's no way. You don't even know me."

Instead of responding, Spade switched the subject.

As he dove into the topic of what it was like to run his clubs, I listened as if he was presenting a lecture and everything I needed to know was in every word he uttered. The passion for which he displayed when it came to his clubs told me that he took pride in his businesses. He wasn't just a man looking to have a name for himself. He was a man looking to thrive in society.

"Is that why you're getting your degree?"

He shot me a sheepish look. "Getting my degree has everything to do with Mr. and Mrs. Graham."

I chuckled.

"While they love the fact that their eldest son is able to financially support them, they'd rather I be a college graduate with a normal day to day career. Originally, my mama wasn't too happy that I wanted to open a club. However, considering that it kept me off the streets, she took the lesser of two evils. To her, the club life is way too hectic for a man who wants to have a wife and children someday."

Blinking, I didn't know where to begin with my questioning without coming across as intrusive.

Spade grinned. "Just ask; I see it all over ya face."

"I'm sure you've come across plenty of women in your years..."

He grunted.

"In all those women, you didn't see one of them being your wife?"

His eyebrows lifted in mirth. "You say that as if I've been with every woman I've laid eyes on, Mila."

"I'm sure not *every* one of them, but..."

Spade studied me as he reached for his drink. "Not all women who've had the pleasure of my time, has had the pleasure of experiencing me whether physically, mentally, or both."

Clearing my throat past the unexpected lump that formed there, I said, "That doesn't answer my question."

"I'll do you one better," he responded. He threw back the contents of his glass, grimacing from the sting of the dark liquid, then sat it aside.

"Before I was too wise to understand, I was fuckin' every female I could get my hands on."

I rolled my eyes but didn't interrupt him.

"A good ass nut was all a woman could get from me. I wasn't lookin' for a wife, only my next release. For a very long time things have been different with how I move. I found that the more I stayed to myself, the clearer my mind became, and the more sex wasn't all I looked for in a woman."

"What changed your way of thinking?" I questioned to which he tilted his head and let his eyes roam over me.

"A woman who had the most beautiful smile I'd ever seen caught my attention. My intentions were to dip as soon as the service was over, but I made it my business to be in this woman's space if only for a minute. I told her how fuckin' sexy she was, and the look in her eyes told me that my words fell on curious ground."

Spade bringing up that day brought in a flood of memories. He read me like a well-rehearsed scripture.

"She had a nigga, though. Being the gentleman that I was, I allowed her nigga to live, and got the fuck up outta there before I changed my mind."

I let a second pass before I cackled. "*Gentleman*?"

He laughed too.

"If it wasn't for Darren, you would've stood there and continued to instigate something. I saw it in your..."

Spade licked his lips and smirked knowingly. "Yeah, exactly," he said.

"Anyway," I replied. "You can't possibly expect me to believe that I had anything to do with you wanting to settle down.

"Ever since I laid eyes on you, you've ruined me for any other woman."

I laughed. "*Before* me, Spade," I clarified. "A man with everything you have to offer a woman should be settled down, married, with a few children *already*."

"I could say the same for a woman like you," he shot back.

"You're deflecting."

"I apologize," he smoothly remarked. "The answer is just as simple as I've already supplied, Mila. Is it so hard to understand that I want, or better yet *crave*, you. You're sittin' across from a man that's been around, seen a lot of beautiful women. Shit like that doesn't excite me. What excites me is a woman's walk, her confidence, her ability to command my attention, her ability to make me wanna do things I've never done before. *This* woman inhales and exhales every particle of my being. She's intelligent, strong-willed, and dangerous as fuck when it comes to one simple look from her beautiful ass eyes. I never met that woman, until you."

Digesting everything he said took a minute. Spade had a way with words, which I knew. His assignments were always top tier which is why his ass was top in my class.

"So, you've been a virgin since we first met?"

He chortled. "Just 'cause I fuck a woman, doesn't mean I wanna be with her. I'm tryna be with you. Fuckin' you is just an added bonus that I'll take great pleasure in."

"Well," I sighed. "Let me help you out—we can't be together. This weekend is all that I'm offering, and afterwards, I'd appreciate it if we pretend like it never happened."

"Damn," he commented with a gentle smile. "I see how callous that shit sounds." Shrugging, he continued, "If all I have is this weekend, I intend to make sure you leave wanting to come back before you even make it out of the driveway."

Help me, I thought.

"Yeah, you betta pray for help," he chimed, reading my mind. "I gotta make these few days worth it."

Help me!

I grabbed my flute and downed my champagne hoping it would alleviate the heat rising in my middle.

"So, tell me what you prefer?"

"As in?"

"Pleasure."

Shit! He's making it worse!

"It's been a while," I croaked.

He smiled.

"What do *you* prefer?" I questioned in return.

Without hesitation, he replied, "I prefer pleasin' you."

"Answer's too broad," I stated although my body melted.

"So was yours," he quipped. "However, since you asked, I'll be generous and explain." Moving the table that separated us aside, he came closer, leaning into my space.

"I prefer eatin', bitin', suckin'...watchin' my dick slide in and outta you, *every part of you.* I prefer hearin' ya cries of pleasure from whichever way I decide to fuck you up." He seemed to growl, while I guess I shouldn't have pried.

Spade's hand spanned the width of my thigh and then some as he grabbed me and positioned me over his lap, making me straddle him. His face rested perfectly in front of my titties. The crotch of my panties was already moist from our back and forth and being this close to his dick caused my core to clinch.

"Let's just kiss, aight?" he mumbled before dropping a peck on the swell of my right breast. What was it with these pecks?

"Kiss?" I questioned breathlessly. What the hell was a kiss going to do? The way my body was on fire, I wanted him buried deep inside of me. Hell, he sat here talking all that freaky shit and now all he wanted to do was kiss!

"Hmm, hm," he confirmed. "There's a lot of passion in kissin', shawty. So, I don't do it or take it lightly."

He started with gentle kisses along my breasts. His hands trailed from my thighs to my ass, igniting everything from my toes to my scalp. When his fingers slipped inside the back of my boy shorts to roughly cup my cheeks, I tilted my head back and moaned. Seconds later I felt his teeth sink into the flesh of right breast.

"Ssss..." The pain felt so good.

Spade's tongue slithered down my skin until his teeth moved the fabric aside. I could do nothing but gasp as he flicked my erect nipple, making it harder. He slid me up on his lap until my box rested on his stiffness. He paid my other nipple the same attention before sucking on it, bringing my whole breast into his mouth.

My hips jerked, grinding on him as my pussy thumped. My skin prickled when his fingers ran along the seam of my ass, scorching me.

"You're beautiful, Professor," he mumbled against my lips.

I held on to his shoulders, sinking my fingers into his glorious skin as he placed wet kisses over my neck. He was at my lips again, sucking and biting them while growling. His hands left my ass and dove into my hair gripping handfuls of my roots as he devoured me in a kiss that shook me to the core. He commanded my tongue in a way that left me dizzy and had me begging for more.

And he gave it to me, kissing me senseless.

I sucked his tongue in return, drawing praise from his lips. His voice and the friction of him beneath me sent my middle quivering in response. I gasped into his mouth as an orgasm overtook me.

Spade's chuckle, although devilish, stirred my soul. As I stared into his aroused, low-set eyes, I realized I'd never look at kissing the same after what he'd just done to me.

CHAPTER 5

GRIM

Mila's body was soft as hell. As she slept, I cocooned her freshly washed body with mine. Inwardly, I smiled as she snuggled even closer. The orgasm she experienced had her so weak that once we hit the bed, she was out like a light. I could only imagine how good she'd feel after I drained her body dry.

At this point, Mila could squash all that shit about us not being together beyond the weekend. After she just came off of us kissing, wasn't a thing in hell that was going to keep me from staking my claim on her ass.

Over the past few months, something within me snapped. Snapped like, I'd make it to where no other nigga wanted to come behind me. I'd have Mila so fucked up in the head that every nigga she came in contact with would know exactly what my mouth and dick did to her.

I came across as being crazy about Mila, because I was. The feelings I had for her had too much time to grow and settle within me. It was all I could do to sit in her class and pay attention without daydreaming about us waking up next to each other. If it wasn't for the way she interrupted my days by owning my thoughts, I wouldn't be feeling half the shit that I felt.

Telling her I was in love with her was probably too soon. She looked at my ass like I was crazy. It didn't upset me that she laughed it off. I intended to show her in every way better than I could tell her.

Sometimes people had to realize that love had no specific date on it. Doing everything to try and reason why being in love wasn't possible took more time than accepting that love exists, and that it was possible to feel it even if you don't understand the how or why. Hell, for all I knew I fell in love with Mila at first sight. That was the only explanation I had for why I'd been spending the last three years of my life waiting for her.

Morning arrived with me waking Mila up to kisses and breakfast in bed. While she ate, I coaxed her into taking a walk with me along the beach. She declined at first, for fear someone would see the two of us together. The sting of annoyance quickly passed, as I produced one of my basketball hats. It covered her face just enough. With it on, she still looked sexy as hell.

She dressed in cutoff shorts and a simple white tank top. Her nipples that I'd sucked and bit on last night poked through her shirt, begging for me to have them again. Swallowing back the lust I felt, I ushered Mila out of the patio door so that we could start our walk.

It wasn't quite ten, the sun wasn't high in the sky, yet the gentle breeze that wrapped us in its fingers was more warm than cool.

"It's beautiful out here," she commented as we descended the stairs. Big waves crashed heavily along the shore as if a storm was on the horizon. Putting my nose to the air, I inhaled a lungful of air. Rain would come this weekend.

Catching her hand in mine, I said, "As beautiful as it is, I'm sure you would've loved my other house instead." We walked just out of reach of the water, so that our shoes wouldn't get wet.

"Where is it?" she asked.

"Back in the city, but on the outskirts."

"Oh," she remarked. "I bet it's beautiful."

"It is," I confirmed. "I'll get you a key for that door too."

Mila's head whipped my way, sending her hair flying. If it wasn't for the hat, the thick strands would've torn her face up.

"Speaking of keys," she said. "I'm sure there are a lot of other ones floating around this region."

I busted out laughing bringing a big smile to her face. "Hell, nah, it ain't! The fuck I look like givin' access to my shit like that, baby?"

"You gave access to me," she pointed out.

"That ain't help ya case, shawty."

She rolled her eyes and smirked.

"You gon' soon realize I'm not playin' witchu," I decreed.

Mila snickered. "Whatever, Spade."

"And that *Spade* shit definitely gotta get the fuck on."

She cracked up. Since she thought it was funny I lifted her off her feet and darted toward the water.

"No, okay!" she cried laughing and clutched my shoulders for dear life.

I placed her back on her feet right as the waves came crashing ashore.

"Ahh!" She hauled ass trying to beat the water from nipping at her Nike slides.

I balled over laughing, then regretted it when she came flying towards me and hopped on me like I was a female half her size instead of a grown ass man twice her size.

"Grr!" she growled and swung on me until I hemmed her little ass up.

Bear hugging her from the back, I made sure to lock her arms down so she wouldn't get free.

As she squealed, I asked, "You gon' stop callin' me Spade?"

She laughed harder but didn't give in. I walked us back toward the water causing her to screech with laughter.

"Okay! Okay!" she acquiesced through a series of giggles.

"What's my name?"

"Grim!" she reluctantly declared.

"I'm glad we came to a mutual understanding." I kissed her cheek, let her go, and took her hand back into mine. This was the type of shit that couples did. Although I was a fairly serious man, everything didn't have to be serious. I woke up this morning light on my feet and giddy because of the woman lying in my bed. With everything in me, I was going to find a way to keep her close.

"So, how're your clubs managing without you this weekend?" she asked after a few minutes had passed.

"Kain is the manager of both clubs. I have two other men under him who help out when the need arises."

"So, how does Kain balance being married and running your clubs?"

Smiling, because she was thinking about what I told her yesterday, I replied, “Like an Olympic gold medalist. He and his wife, Tawny, have a wonderful relationship.” I was proud of each of my brothers for where they were in their lives and relationships. Hopefully, I’d soon join their club.

As we made our way farther down the beach, bypassing early beach goers, Mila held my hand a little tighter and ducked her head.

We approached the pier, which I led us on. The pier was lively as it always was on the weekends. It didn’t matter what time of day it was, this was the one part of the beach that would be teeming with activity. Booths were set up along the stretch of pier, offering everything from skin products to custom paintings and portraits.

“Lord,” Mila mumbled. “This is too high off the ground, Grim,” she said, nervously glancing back and forth between me and the pier’s wooden railing as if she was too afraid to go near the edge. “I can’t swim,” she told me.

“And you think I’d let anything happen to you?”

She smacked her pretty teeth. “You have no loyalty to me. Hypothetically speaking, if I was to somehow end up over those rails, there’s no reason for you to jump behind me and save me.”

I scoffed. “Damn, you just made me sound lame as fuck.”

She snickered. "It's the truth, though."

"It isn't," I countered. "Ya safety is my number one priority, Professor."

"Really? Don't call me that out here," she chastised in a hushed tone.

I barked with laughter. "I could put you up against those rails, make love to you, and wouldn't a soul say or do shit about it. No one's payin' attention to us."

She tsked. "That's not true." She motioned her head towards a group of women heading our way and staring at us. A couple of their faces were familiar, but I couldn't call them by name. Clad in barely there bikinis, the melanin rich queens were fine as hell. Living on the beach, I saw this shit all the time, so a naked body didn't move me one way or the other. My concern walked next to me, gripping my hand like the pier would collapse beneath us.

Grinning, I shrugged. "We're a sexy ass couple, baby."

She grumbled in reply.

Women forgotten, Mila pointed out a booth which had several African themed accessories on display. She tugged me along as she admired a patterned scarf hanging from a display rack. I guess she forgot about not wanting to be seen. Glad that she was loosening up, I didn't utter a word.

"This is beautiful!" She ran her fingers over the soft, colorful fabric and did the same with another scarf hanging behind it.

"Those are handmade. No two designs are alike," the brown-skinned sister sitting behind the table stated with a smile. The man sitting beside her casually nodded as he typed away on a laptop perched on his lap. I saw them a few times while walking along the pier. While she tended to her customers, he'd be dividing his attention between her and his laptop.

"I want both of these," Mila said.

"Those are her favorites," the guy stated, grinning.

The lady shushed him. "Pay him no mind. I let him come out here with me every so often, and now he thinks he can start minding my business." She and Mila busted out laughing while me and dude side-eyed them.

"Would you mind holding them while I run back to get my purse?" Mila asked.

"Of course, no problem!" The lady nodded and smiled as Mila handed her the scarves. Reaching into the pocket of my cargo shorts, I produced my wallet.

"She'll take them now," I said, handing her cash. She smiled, handed me my change, and placed the scarves in a brown paper bag bearing her logo.

Mila took her bag with a gracious smile.

"Thank you for stopping by and shopping with me," the lady beamed.

"You didn't have to, Grim. Thank you," Mila said as we walked away from the booth and continued down the pier.

Forty bucks wasn't anything to me, so I chuckled. "Next time I take you shoppin' at least try to break the bank," I quipped.

She rolled her eyes and bit into her lip to keep from smiling.

We continued walking until we reached the end of the pier.

"This view is amazing," she mentioned. When I tried walking closer to the rail, she stopped me.

"I thought I told you that you're safe with me," I stated. "Come here."

Hesitantly, she allowed me to bring her to the wooden rails. I positioned her in front of me, then wrapped my arms around her middle.

"See, it's not so bad," I mumbled against her neck before placing a kiss there. Her heart beat raced a mile a minute, prompting me to say, "Enjoy the view, baby. These arms around you won't let go."

She relaxed against my chest and marveled at the view.

"You get to see this every day?"

"When I'm here."

She took a deep breath, then exhaled.

"You can have this view whenever you want," I told her.

Her expression was one of whimsy. "What don't you understand about this only being for the weekend?"

Kissing up her neck, I ignored her comment. She could feel how she wanted to, and so could I. Just to remind her of who the fuck I was, I turned her until she faced me, then dropped my lips to hers. A nigga could never kiss her like I could. She knew that shit too, moaning as I sucked on her tongue and clutched her ass in these short ass shorts she had on.

A tap on my shoulder interrupted our kiss.

"You two are beautiful together. I hope you don't mind." It was the lady from the table where Mila purchased her scarves. She handed me a photo taken with one of those old school Polaroid cameras. The photo was of Mila and me.

"Moments like these should be cherished. Y'all have a nice day." She smiled and left just as quietly as she came.

"How sweet," Mila said as she looked at the photo. She took it from me and slid it into the bag with the scarves. "Too bad it has to be destroyed."

“Why. Our faces aren’t showin’,” I protested with my face balled up.

She shrugged.

I was half tempted to act a fool on this pier, but I had to remember that this was her weekend, one I intended for her to enjoy. If that meant letting her believe what she wanted to believe, then so be it. Come Sunday, all bets were off, and Mila would understand just how serious I was about her.

After we’d had our fill of the morning’s beauty, Mila jumped on my back and requested that I carry her back to the house. I did so with ease. She was made for my arms, for me to carry, and for me to seduce until she fell hard as fuck for me.

Back in the house, Mila retreated to the bathroom while I went into the kitchen to make us a drink. Ten minutes later, Mila appeared in the kitchen, refreshed. I handed her the glass of tea I had poured her, leaned against the counter, and sipped my beer.

She studied me for a minute, then uttered, “Truth or dare.”

"Truth."

"Are you into illegal activities?"

A smirk tugged at my lips. "I hope you understand what you're asking, Mila. Answerin' questions like this comes with a price."

"You chose truth," was her response.

"Occasionally," I answered.

"Why?"

"One question, shawty."

Rolling her eyes, she said, "Dare."

"Let me record everything we do," I responded.

Her eyes bucked. "Hell, no!"

I chuckled, rounded the island to where she stood, and tapped the shorts she wore.

"Take 'em off," I demanded.

She gasped. "I didn't say anything about playing this stupid game, Grim."

"You didn't say anything about rules either, Mila. I asked you could I dare you, and you said yes. There are repercussions when a dare isn't accepted. You know that, right?"

She glared at me, then reluctantly unbuttoned her shorts and slipped out of them. Her thick hips taunted me to take them in my hands, but I refrained for now.

I went back to my side of the island and picked up my drink.

"Truth," I said.

She shook her head. "I don't want to play this game with you, Grim."

Grinning, I asked, "You scared?"

She still had not gotten the full answer she sought in the first place. I loved that I was learning Mila so quickly. Knowing she wouldn't let it go, I waited for her to ask.

"Why do anything that's illegal? You don't care about jeopardizing everything?"

I tilted my head in thought. "I can't jeopardize everything, when everything isn't tied to money. A person should be more concerned about *who* they'd lose 'cause of their lifestyle."

"So, is that to say you're not concerned about your loved ones?"

"Lil baby," I chuckled. My eyes skipped to her tank top. "Truth or dare."

"Dare," she hesitantly said.

Surprised she didn't choose truth, I said, "Same as before."

She shook her head.

"Strip," I casually ordered.

She removed her tank top, dropping it to the floor. Her titties, still bound by a bra, peeked from the lace cups.

"Truth," I issued, while remembering how I'd sucked on her nipples last night.

"Why do you keep choosing truth?"

"Is that your question?" Done with the lemonade, I pushed the pitcher aside, and moved on to cleaning the mess I'd made.

"No," she quickly answered. "Aren't you concerned about your loved ones? Your woman?"

"My family is everything to me," I replied. "These days I'm more removed than I am involved with anything...illegal. I get my hands dirty if necessary." I didn't elaborate, letting her imagination take her wherever she wanted to go.

Her imagination must've dropped her off on Elm Street, because she stared at me wide-eyed, shuddered for no reason, then cleared her throat.

"Dare," she croaked.

Hm. I found that interesting.

"The dare won't change."

Huffing, she removed the hair tie from her ponytail sending her hair falling around her shoulders. My eyes shimmered with heat.

"Truth," I said, then caught my lip between my teeth. She stood across the island looking like I'd just fucked her.

"Do you have any kids?"

"If I did, they'd be here with me."

"You're cheating," she griped.

"Am not," I defended.

"How is it you're fully clothed while I'm standing here in my bra and panties?"

Shrugging, I replied, "You should be standin' there in nothing if you ask me."

Her eyes narrowed.

"It's truth or dare, baby girl. If you don't carry out the dares you keep requesting or give up the truths you wish not to divulge... I can't help that."

She winced. "You've dared me to do the same thing three times."

Shrugging, I flicked my eyes at her pebbled nipples poking against the bra before returning my gaze to hers. "It's a simple dare, Mila."

She shook her head. "It isn't, though. You want to record everything we do. The idea is that no one knows I'm here. We've already crossed that line with your brothers. And on the pier, it completely slipped my mind that I was supposed to be incognito. You didn't even bring it to my attention."

The only comment I wanted to address was the one about recording us. "Are you implying that I'd show others what we'll be doin' to each other?"

She nodded.

"There's just one problem: I'm a stingy ass muhfucka. Did you forget that I said I don't like to share? The recordings will be for my own pleasure, and yours. According to you, this weekend is all I have with you. I have to hold on to those memories somehow."

"Yes," she stated. "In that brain of yours that can retain all of the other shit you know."

Laughing, I remarked, "Nah, I need more than that. The idea is also that we explore each other without inhibitions. I want to record every single time we make love—"

"Fuck," she interrupted.

"It'll definitely be both," I smoothly replied.

She smacked her teeth.

"Or else, what is the point of takin' the risk to be here with me?"

"Maybe coming here was a bad idea," she quipped. Now she was about to piss me off.

Smirking, I sauntered up to her. My fingers trailed across her shoulder, causing her to shiver before I gently cupped her throat. She gasped. I felt her pulse quicken as I turned her around. Standing behind her, I tilted her head so that she could look into my eyes.

"I can promise you, I'm the best anything you'll ever have."

Mila's eyes glazed over.

"So, it's up to you to trust me. Will you allow yaself to do nothin' but let me cater to you, make love to you, fuck you, and please you as often as ya pussy gets wet?"

She bit into her bottom lip, prompting me to lower my head and take over. While I kept one hand around her throat, the other skimmed down to allow my fingers to tweak her erect nipple.

"Mmm..." she moaned and rubbed against my hard dick. Her scent found me, causing me to brick up even more.

"See," I teased. "She's ready for me just that quickly." I licked along her neck and continued to toy with her nipple before my fingers left her bra and searched lower. Slipping my fingers inside her black, lace panties, I groaned at the wetness that met my digits.

"Good and wet," I praised. She shuddered as my fingers spread her lips and met the hardened bud begging for me. Gently pinching it, I got exactly what I wanted. Juices flowed from her, soaking her panties as she panted.

Damn, I hadn't even started.

"Let me record this moment, baby. Whenever you need to be reminded of how good I fucked you, all you gotta do is press play." I plunged my fingers into her tight wet center and growled at the way she clinched around them.

"Yes!" Her body shook as she came around my dancing fingers. The way she gasped for air had my dick swollen to the point I had to grit my teeth from the pressure.

Pulling back, I slid my fingers from her tunnel and immediately licked them clean while holding her weak body with my other arm. Because she faltered a little, I picked her up, and let her wrap her legs around me.

I made it to the bedroom, deposited her atop the bed, then backtracked to the dresser where my remotes were. Picking the one that controlled my cameras, I turned them on with a simple click of a button.

Moving back toward the bed, I ripped my shirt off and shucked my shorts off in the process. Mila lay strewn across the bed, eyes glazed, panties wet, and bra halfway off as she eyed my swinging dick. The bed dipped under my weight as I kissed her right ankle and trailed my lips up her leg, thigh, and to the seam of her panties.

As soon as my tongue dragged up her encased pussy, she jerked. Moving her panties aside, I let my tongue play with her wet sex, teasing her just a bit. She spread her thighs more, welcoming me to have my way.

"Grim," she begged as her hand fell to my head.

Ripping the delicate garment from her body, I went back in, devouring her middle wrenching a loud moan from her lips. She tasted so good that I moaned against her sex and latched onto her nub. Her thighs shook uncontrollably as I sucked her into a nut that I lapped up like I hadn’t eaten in days. I gave her another one just so I could savor her flavor again.

I kissed my way north, stopping at her swollen nipples. I swear, Mila had nipples that a nigga could suck on just for the fuck of it. She brought my lips to hers, feverishly kissing me.

My heavy dick strained to be inside of her, so I led him straight there.

“Ooohhh!” she gasped.

“Fucckk,” I echoed. Gritting my back teeth, I pushed into Mila until I was buried deep inside of her. She suffocated my length, drawing a moan of admiration from me.

Pushing her thighs back, I dropped my head into the crevice of her neck, pulled back, then slowly pushed forward.

“Griiimmm!” she groaned.

Shit! Every part of me that waited for this moment wasn’t prepared for how fucking good this woman felt.

“Every class, I sit there and imagine fuckin’ you ‘til you scream my name,” I admitted.

She cooed as I hit a spot that had her gripping me tighter. Her hands smoothed up my back until I felt her fingernails biting into my flesh.

"Do you imagine me inside you, Mila?"

"Shiitt, yes!" she mumbled as her eyes rolled. Tears trickled from her closed lids, sparking my blood.

"Open ya eyes, baby," I requested. She opened them just barely. I turned her head showing her the camera I'd installed on the headboard. The angle was perfect.

"I'ma replay the way you nuttin' all over my dick as much as I fuckin' want to."

I dipped deeper, grunting when she convulsed around my dick. My heart raced from exhilaration. Mila's thighs which I had cocked open and pushed back became the prey that my teeth sought out as I sucked and bit all over them while I dug her out. The fact that she met my strokes damn near killed me.

"Griimm!" she breathlessly shouted as her pussy clamped down on me.

"Fuck!" I growled, feeling my body tense.

Seconds later, she wailed my name again and came so hard that I had to snatch out to keep from spraying my nut inside her tunnel. Instead, I gripped my dick and shot my seed all over her titties and abdomen.

Yall are stupid! Nobody's pull out game is that strong

CHAPTER 6

MILA

Sometime later my eyes drifted open. The sun had faded, leaving the room cast in soft light from the bedside lamp. My gaze darted to the camera on the headboard as shame tinted my cheeks.

"Shit," I mumbled. Body naked and tired, I carefully maneuvered out of the bed.

On the dresser lay a pair of silk, red panties, and a white tank top. I made my way to the bathroom before remembering Spade and I had already bathed. Well, he'd bathed me as I lay against his chest, exhausted from the way he'd drained my body.

My middle purred in spite of the yawn that tripped from my lips. My phone was next to the clothes, blinking.

I sighed and called Kai back.

"Just checkin' on you, sis," she answered. "Making sure he didn't kill yo' ass."

Grimacing, I donned my clothes while saying, "I'm never going to forgive you and Lucy for talking me into this shit. Grim-I mean *Spade* is—"

"*Grim*!" Kai chortled. "Oh, sis, it's like *that*?"

"No!" I denied.

My heart thudded. I couldn't go back to calling him Spade. Everything about him screamed *Grim* and as such, I'd call him by the name he wished to go by. Shaking my head, I balked at myself. All it took was for Grim to drop his dick in me and now I was around here bowing to his wishes.

"You know they say the best sex is with someone it's not supposed to be with," her country ass jeered.

"Kai!" I scoffed at the same time as I heard Kai's husband's voice.

"Don't let ya mouth get you fucked up, Kai," Chuck warned.

"Baby, I was talkin' to Mila," she explained. "You know what I'm saying is true. Look at us," she smoothed over.

Chuck grumbled something incoherent as Kai went back to talking.

"Mila if you don't let your hair down and enjoy this weekend, I'm going to disown you. I was telling Chuck about you and Grim—"

"Kai, no!" I fussed, embarrassed.

"Girl, whatever! Chuck wasn't even surprised. He said Grim asks about you all the time."

My eyebrows scrunched together. "Why didn't Chuck ever say anything?"

Kai sighed. "He said he wasn't about to let Grim waste your time. Isn't my man thoughtful?" Kai gushed.

"He is," I agreed. Chuck, although heavy in the streets, was a good man to my best friend. They'd gotten married against her parent's wishes, however Kai wouldn't have changed her decision for anything. She and Chuck fit each other perfectly, and I loved the way he loved her.

Seeing their relationship blossom, as well as Lucy and Darren's relationship blossom made me want to try love again. Especially on those nights when I was lonely as hell—which was often.

While I complained about being lonely, I did enjoy the peace I found. When I used to get home from work just to be his verbal punching bag for whatever he'd gone through at work drained me to the point of numbness. Still, I'd listen to him bitch about his day without complaining. After all, I was his woman. If I couldn't be a listening ear, another woman would.

When his agitation and anger increased, I found myself staying late at work just to avoid going home. That made no sense. A woman should come home and feel welcomed, sheltered, and loved in her environment. Instead, I experienced the worst kind of emotional neglect. Every day I did my best to encourage him, but my words had repeatedly fallen on deaf ears. While I was busy trying to nurture him, he was sucking the life out of me. After all I'd put up, Amir still had the audacity to cheat on me.

"You know what, Kai, you're right," I mumbled. "I need to loosen up and enjoy myself."

Grim put me to sleep a little while ago, so that should've been all the confirmation I needed to realize I *was* enjoying myself with him. Being with him on the pier felt like I was on a walk with my real man. I remembered the pressure of his hand holding mine, and the way he held me in his arms while we overlooked the water.

His kisses were my undoing. Should Grim ever make a woman his, I'd envy her for the simple fact that she'd get to feel his lips every day. That man knew how to work his mouth, that was all to it.

Besides the fact that what we were doing was forbidden, it didn't keep me from wanting Grim inside of me again and kissing me again.

Just then I heard his boisterous laughter. I heard the chef's familiar voice, prompting me to ball my face up.

Why couldn't Grim understand that I didn't want *anyone* seeing me here? There was no turning back from us sleeping together, but we could still avoid being caught if he'd just follow my directions.

"I'm glad you see things my way, sis," Kai said. "I'm going to call Lucy and let her know you're still breathing. We can't wait to hear what he has in store for tomorrow."

"I'm not looking forward to anything." Being with Amir taught me not to look forward to my birthday. "If I get a 'happy birthday' from him, I'll be fine. It'll be more than I've had from any man in a while."

Kai smacked her teeth. "Just take pictures so Lucy and I can pretend like we spent the day with you," she requested.

"Yeah, sure," I responded.

"Love you, boo!" Kai stated. I issued her the same sentiment before we disconnected.

I also had messages from my mother, which I answered then sat the phone back on the dresser.

As tired as my body was, I wanted to lay back down. In protest, my stomach growled at the smell of the food, moving my feet out of the room. Because I was barely dressed, I backtracked to the dresser and pulled out a pair of Grim's sweats and a t-shirt before making my way out of the room.

Tiptoeing down the stairs, I wanted to see if Grim was in eyesight. He stood in the entrance of the kitchen, bowl in hand as he bit into a piece of melon and laughed at something the chef said. Grim was shirtless, in his signature cargo shorts, and barefoot. His heavily tattooed chest and back were built to perfection, causing me to stare.

He must've sensed me, because I was too quiet for him to have heard me approaching. His blazing eyes trailed my frame as though I was naked, then he beckoned me over. I shook my head. Although the chef prepared dinner for us yesterday, I hadn't once laid eyes on him.

Grim nodded and beckoned me once again. Hesitantly, I proceeded toward him. He took my hand and led me into the kitchen, where I was taken aback by the man standing at the kitchen island preparing two thick steaks for the grill. *The chef* didn't look anything like I expected him to.

"Mila, meet my cousin Choppa," Grim introduced all the while lifting me to place me on the counter.

Choppa smiled revealing straight white teeth. "Evenin', Mila," he spoke.

Clearing my throat of the uncertainty clogging it, I replied, "Hey."

Grim stepped between my legs and grabbed my attention with a simple kiss to my forehead. He placed at piece of melon at my lips. Without hesitation, I bit into it. He popped the other half into his mouth.

"How was ya nap?" he asked.

Blushing, I replied, "Fine."

"Just 'fine'?" he teased while biting into another piece of fruit. He offered me the other half, which I gracefully ate from his fingers.

"Damn... 'For the night's over with, I'ma have to do better."

My cheeks blazed with fire causing him to chuckle. Grim surprised me with how romantic and playful he was. I needed him to be rude and bad in bed, so that I could forget this weekend ever happened. Instead, I was on a fast track to binding my soul with his.

Two hours later, Grim and I finished dinner and retired to his bedroom with drinks and dessert. I placed our drinks on the nightstand, stripped of the sweats and t-shirt, then stretched. My body was still sore, many muscles aching from lack of use. Mid-stretch, Grim's hands smoothed up my back and over my shoulders, applying firm pressure.

"Let me handle this for you," he said.

I crawled onto the bed and lay on my stomach, dessert forgotten.

Grim laughed as he joined me on the bed. I thought I'd feel his hands, so when I felt his lips touch the back of my right thigh, I jerked.

"You know what I noticed about you this evenin', baby?" His lips continued up my thigh until he'd reached my butt.

"What?" I asked breathlessly. Aroused, I squirmed to squelch the pulsing in my core.

"I noticed that ya walk is different."

Yes, he was right.

"That shit turns me on like fuck," he uttered as he maneuvered my panties off. Next, I felt the pressure of his hands on the back of my thighs. He kneaded into them drawing a moan from me as I lifted my ass in the air.

Grim kissed my asshole before I felt his tongue there.

"Ooohhh!" I gripped a handful of the blankets as he planted his mouth between my ass cheeks.

Methodically, his hands massaged my thighs as he pleased me in a way I had never been pleased before. I came so hard, tears clouded my eyes. All the while Grim's hands massaged my ass, and lower back as his tongue made it to my dripping center. At the same time as he latched onto my clit, his fingers firmly dug into the muscles of my lower back, bringing my entire body under his submission.

He sucked and moaned against my sex like it was a Slurpee.

"I'ma beat the fuck outta this pussy," he warned.

I came, collapsing against the bed as my body purred.

"Nah, no sleepin'," he said, turning me over. "You can sleep afterwards."

Grim's expression as he loomed over me was one of reverence, and passion. Seeing my juices staining his face caused a tide of emotions to assail my mind. I let my knees fall open as he inhaled each of my titties one at a time.

Greedily, I reached for his dick which hang between his thighs hard, long, and thick, just perfect.

"I can't wait to see these pretty ass lips wrapped around my shit," he uttered against my lips as he slowly entered me, stretching me like crazy. My mouth hung open.

"Damn, baby," he groaned. "I love how this pussy begs for me."

I started begging then. "Grim, please..." I needed him to relieve this pressure building inside of me. If what we were doing wasn't just for the weekend, I'd swear Grim was made for me. At least his dick was. Every time he beat on my spot, I silently fell for him.

I palmed his beard covered jaws and brought his juicy lips to mine. This time, I took over, licking and sucking on his bottom lip while he dug deeper into my wet sex.

My eyes glazed over when he positioned my legs over his shoulders and delivered the longest, deepest strokes I've ever felt. As he moved inside of me all I could think was I couldn't allow this man to make me feel shit that was downright foolish to feel. After tonight, I'd get my head out of the clouds and remember that this was just sex, Grim wasn't my man, and he couldn't be man.

"Fuck, I feel you cummin', baby!"

Yes. Come tomorrow, I'd have my head back on straight. As for right now, I moaned loudly as an orgasm shot me to the stars.

While Grim slept, I crawled out of bed and tiptoed through the moonlit room to find the remote that controlled his cameras. Finding the right button, I pressed it to enable the camera that I needed. I wasn't sure if I was still high off the orgasms he'd given me a little while ago, or if I was just plain crazy, but I needed Grim's dick. Now.

He stirred as I crawled back onto the bed and positioned myself between his thighs. We were both ass naked, having showered after our last session. As if he sensed me near, Grim's dick grew against his thigh.

Taking it into my hands, I stroked him, causing his eyes to pop open, and his dick to fully harden.

Before he could utter a word, I spit on his bulbous head, swirled it around with my tongue, then eased my mouth down his length.

"Mmm..." His precum tasted so good.

"Fuucckk!"

I wasn't expecting Grim to grab my hair the way he did. While rough, I loved it.

"Fuck, Mila," he moaned. "Suck on my shit just like that, baby," he entreated.

Slurp! Slurp!

While my mouth and tongue worked, I used one hand to stroke his length, while the other massaged his heavy balls. I had him sloppy wet and gagged on his tip when I deep throated him. His hips raised off the bed, seeking the sensation I delivered him.

"Mila!" he growled sexily. "I'm cummin'!"

He didn't have to warn me as his breathing pattern changed. I felt his body tense, then repeatedly jerk as his seeds shot off in my mouth. Keeping up, I didn't allow one drop of him to go to waste.

*****

"Happy Birthday, baby girl!" My mom and dad shouted. They were so loud and country that Grim snickered.

Placing my hand over his mouth, I silenced him.

"Thank you!" I responded to my parents with a genuine smile. We were on FaceTime, so I had to school my features. Grim's strong thighs beneath me and his hands resting on my thighs made it complicated. We were out on the deck after enjoying breakfast and in the middle of kissing when my phone rang.

I threatened him to not say a word before answering my mother's call.

"We hate you're not feeling well. We were going to come see you today."

My eyes bucked. "Uhm... No, I'm still...sore." I bit my lip to keep from laughing at Grim's expression.

"Well, dear, just continue soaking—"

I died while Grim scoffed and tried to keep from busting out laughing.

"—and hopefully, you'll feel better by tomorrow. We'll come see you next weekend if that's better for you," my mom said.

Not only was my mother talking in front of my dad, but Grim was going to explode with laughter if I didn't hurry up and get them off the phone.

"Yes, that'll be fine," I answered. "I love you both."

"We love you, dear," my dad replied.

I hung up embarrassed as hell.

"Forget you ever heard that," I stated.

"I won't," he chuckled. "It was pretty funny. And for the record, you've been doin' plenty of soakin', so she's givin' you sound advice."

My face stung with heat. He reached up and pinched my chin. "I hope all ya birthday wishes come true today," he said, warming my heart.

This morning, Grim woke me up, writing happy birthday all over my sex. As far as birthday wishes, I didn't have any. However, Grim hoping the best for me was more than any man had ever given me excluding my father of course.

"Thank you, Grim. I really appreciate—"

"See, you're about to sound like we're strangers or some shit," he said. "I *appreciate* the fact that you're finally callin' me Grim after all these years. What I don't appreciate is you comin' at me like I'm just a fuck."

I cocked my head, confused. "How am I coming at you like that?"

"*'I really appreciate'* sounds like some shit you tell a cashier or someone who just served you dinner—not a nigga that's been knowin' you for two years, and a nigga you finally let fuck you like you need to be fucked." He pushed my chin up to close my mouth which was ajar. "The same nigga that you've been layin' up under like I'm ya nigga. So, which is it? Are we strangers, or are we more than that?"

"Of course, we're more than strangers," I answered. "How else am I supposed to tell you that I appreciate you?"

He shrugged. "Actions speak louder than words." His fingers trailed down my face as he stared into my eyes. "It can be nice to hear, but I need to know you mean that shit."

Something passed through the atmosphere, shaking my soul. It occurred to me that I was in the arms of a man that didn't have to have me here. He wanted me here, in his space, just like this. I underestimated Grim. If I'd ever felt trapped in something, it was now. Because how the hell was I going to detach myself from Grim come tomorrow?

CHAPTER 7

GRIM

Decorators quietly moved about downstairs, while I checked in on Mila to make sure that she was still asleep. I tired her out with a game of water tag in which we had to play in a floatie because she couldn't swim. Water tag turned into me putting her up against the pool wall and her cumming around my dick. It did the trick, though, knocking her ass out.

That was two hours ago. As I peeked in on her, she stirred. Her naked body lay atop the sheets. The thick strands of her hair were strewn all over her head like she'd been fighting in her sleep.

Chuckling, I entered the room just as she rolled over and opened her eyes.

"How long was I sleep?" she questioned.

"Long enough," I remarked. The decorators were nearly done. I had a few items waiting to be delivered but would be here shortly.

"You ready for a bath?"

"I am," she confirmed with a yawn.

"Come on now, shawty," I joked. "It's ya birthday. We have plans, so you gotta wake up."

"Plans?"

I could see the wheels turning in her head.

"Yes; plans," I reiterated.

Instead of further questioning me, she climbed from the bed, took my proffered hand, and walked with me to the bathroom. The small victory resonated deep in my soul. As she stood in the mirror and dealt with her hair, I started the bath, filling the jacuzzi style tub with hot water and added a little vanilla scented bubble bath.

Moving from the tub, I grabbed a lighter from the counter and proceeded to light the candles spread about the bathroom. Mila had just stepped into the water when the doorbell rang.

"Be right back, baby," I told her, then made my way downstairs.

The decorators were packed up and heading out which was perfect timing.

My mama came waltzing into the house with her eyes darting to and fro looking for Mila.

"Where is she?" she questioned excitedly while handing me the garment bag draped across her arm.

"In the bathroom, Ma."

"Well, I'm gon' wait here, so I can meet her." She traipsed her ass to the sofa and sat down.

"Ma," I chuckled. "No, you're not. At least not today."

"Why not?" she huffed.

I went to the sofa and helped her back to her feet.

"Because Ma... It's a long story, aight?"

"I just drove my ass all the way over here to bring *you* a dress, jewelry, and shoes for a woman I haven't so much as heard you speak of. I'm ya mother and I demand to meet her!"

"Precious!" my dad barked, as he came through the front door carrying the rest of the items I'd ordered. "If you'on take ya ass back to the damn car. The man said not today."

My brothers and I were the spitting image of our father. He didn't play the radio with us growing up, yet I still found myself being rebellious. Thankfully, I had the type of parents that never gave up on me.

"Mind your business, Russell. This is between me and my son," my mama said. She crossed her arms over her breast in defiance.

My attention shot between both, waiting to see who would fold first. You could hear a pin drop as they locked eyes.

Mama smacked her teeth and stomped past me, glaring at me in the process. "Don't come to me when you need help," she hissed.

Laughing at her departing back and my father shaking his head, I should've known my mother would be the first to cave. My father treated her like gold and very seldomly put his foot down with her. But when he did…Precious folded.

"Everything's here," he stated as he placed the bags on the sofa. He dapped me and said, "Now let me go smooth this shit over with ya mama."

I busted out laughing, loving the relationship my parents had even after being together for more than three decades.

After they left, I took the bags along with the garment bag up the stairs to my bedroom, then placed them on the bed. I retrieved a blunt from the nightstand and then stripped of my clothes as I headed back to the bathroom.

"Who was at the door?" Mila asked. Cutting down the lights, I allowed the candles I'd lit to illuminate the space.

"Alexa, play Track 2." Seconds later the sounds of smooth R&B filled the bathroom.

I lit the blunt then joined her in the tub, relaxing opposite her. "My parents."

Mila's eyes snapped wide with panic. *"Spade!"*

"Who?" Although quietly issued, my question made its impact. Dragging from the blunt I resisted the urge to grill her.

Deflated, she asked, "Grim, are you trying to set me up?"

Barking with laughter, I hit the blunt once more before placing it aside. I reached into the water and scooped one of her feet up. The minute my thumb dug into her arch, she bit into her bottom lip and moaned. She relaxed against the tub on a satisfied sigh.

"Every time you strut across the classroom in ya heels, I wanna yank ya ass up," I confessed while delivering kisses to her pretty, white-painted toes.

"How the hell do you even pass the tests if you're busy daydreaming?" she lazily questioned.

Drawing her big toe into my mouth, I sucked on it, then smirked when her eyes glossed over.

"I'm intelligent as fuck, professor."

She grinned. "Which means every time you asked for my help, you didn't need it. I called you on it too."

Chuckling, I conceded, "You're right. I had to be strategic."

Giggling, she replied, "Seeing your emails grated my damn skin."

This time I nipped her big toe causing her to snicker. "We both know that's a lie. Seein' my emails made you wet as fuck. Just like the smell of me has you fuckin' yaself most nights." She claimed to hate the smell of weed, but each time I'd smoked around her, she hadn't made the slightest complaint.

Her lids lifted as a smile played along her juicy lips.

"Did you record yaself pleasin' me?" Damn, I hoped she did.

Her cheeks darkened, but she nodded. "Of course."

Pleased, I said, "I love it on you, baby."

"What?" she asked.

"Grim."

*****

Bath complete, I could practically read Mila's mind as she donned the little black, sequined dress that I'd bought her. My taste was impeccable, and the dress fit her like a glove. She'd moisturized her skin, straightened her hair to perfection, and applied makeup to her face. While she looked good enough to eat, and I would, she was quiet and pensive as she dressed.

Honestly, I'd take pensive Mila. Normally, she'd hesitate or question me at every turn. I'd broken her walls down, bringing her to trust me enough to not question my moves, even if she was in her head about it.

Once she'd stepped into her heels, I sidled up behind her and placed a kiss on the nape of her neck.

"As always, you're beautiful," I complimented, but I'd never stop telling her so.

She turned her smiling eyes to mine. "Thank you," she said as her hands smoothed down the red Polo shirt I wore. "I love this color on you. And, of course, you're the most handsome man I've ever known."

Surprised that she'd uttered those words, I stumbled over what to say. Never did I find myself speechless, and I'd been on the receiving end of several multi-million dollar deals.

Chuckling, she cupped my jaws with her delicate hands. "I'm glad we met, Grim."

Yet another confession that stirred my soul. I found my tongue and finally replied, "So am I." I was rewarded with the taste of her lips.

"You ready?" I asked.

Deeply sighing, she ducked her head. "Ready."

Taking her hand, I led her out of the room. Halfway down the stairs, she gasped.

"Grim!" she exclaimed. She let go of my hand and took off down the stairs like she wasn't in five-inch heels.

Grinning, I reached the bottom of the stairs and asked, "You like?"

In awe, Mila turned slowly as she stood in the middle of the living room floor with her mouth ajar and her eyes wide. The setting was perfect as the sun had faded a while ago and the cast of shadows from the curtain lights bathed us in intimacy.

White, pink, and champagne-colored decorations transformed my living room into a party just for me and her. Most of the furniture had been moved to make way for the dinner table, chairs, and the dance floor which was littered with pink rose petals.

I wanted to make this night special for Mila—even if it had to take place in the living room.

The doorbell rang, drawing me to the door. I let Choppa in and dapped him.

"You might as well book me for the reception, bruh," he commented.

"Shiiidd, you speakin' it into existence," I replied.

"Ain't nothin' wrong with that. If I'm goin' all out for shawty, you best believe she worth it," he said. He hauled his bags in and headed straight for the kitchen.

"You're right," I called to his back. He chuckled.

Back in the living room, Mila was still in the same spot, staring at the spot where her gifts were placed.

“Mila—"

She turned to face me. "You did all of this?"

Nodding, I said, "Kai and Lucy came through also." If it was one thing I could say about her best friends, they were loyal as fuck to Mila. The three of us exchanged several emails over the last few days, making sure I got everything Mila would want.

I wiped her tears bringing her to apologize.

"No apologies needed, sweetheart. As long as they're happy tears, I can accept a few of them."

She stepped into my arms and rested her head against my chest.

"Thank you, Grim," she whispered tearfully. "This is more than I could ever imagine."

I lifted her chin until she and I locked gazes. "Imagine more, baby girl. A weekend won't do justice for what I'd love to do for you."

Her eyes searched mine, and in that moment, I recognized surrender there.

"I see what you feel, Mila. Trust yaself to have it."

She blinked, then shifted her gaze away. Deciding not to push, I swallowed the rejection I felt and motioned to the table holding her gifts. "Open ya gifts.”

With a timid yet gracious smile, she stepped from my embrace.

Every gift occupying the table was from me. Thanks to Kai and Lucy, each gift was chosen with care—like the diamond bracelet that fit her dainty wrist perfectly. She gawked at it, enamored by its beauty. So it was with the two pairs of diamond earrings she opened next. One was a pair of hoops, the other studs to fit the second set of holes in her ears. Next came the Christian Louboutin studded heels that Kai informed me were on Mila's radar.

With each gift her reactions proved that she was beyond grateful, even down to the furry socks she opened next. A few outfits, another pair of heels, makeup, and an envelope of blue faces later, Mila finally spoke.

"This is...amazing," she whispered.

Reaching for her hand, I brought her to my chest.

"Happy Birthday, love," I said, then kissed her forehead and embraced her in a tight hug.

Our hug led us into a slow dance as the track changed to a Miguel joint. I held her close, never wanting this time with her to end. In my mind, things wouldn't end. However, I couldn't force anything with Mila. She had to want us for herself, despite what the fuck kept us apart. I was willing to do whatever needed to be done to keep her. She had to understand that.

"I'm ashamed to say that I've never slow-danced with anyone before." she said jarring me back to reality.

"There's no need to be ashamed," I said. "The man who had you and never led you in a dance should be ashamed."

Her eyes softened. If Mila decided to bite the bullet and say fuck it just to be with me, I'd give her the world. Teaching was important to her, and I hated to feel like her career didn't mean shit over what we could have. But that's exactly how I felt—selfish as fuck over this woman.

Drop out, problem solved
Finish somewhere else

*****

And no one does it like me
And no one but you
Has that kind of whip appeal on me

Damn, this Baby Face joint never hit as hard as it did now. Mila and I were done with dinner and were sharing another dance. She had her head buried in my neck while my arms enveloped her, sealing us together.

She'd been unusually quiet as we ate, leaving me to wonder what was on her mind. Tonight, was the last night we had together according to her, and truthfully, a small part of me warned me to be ready for whatever tomorrow held, but I ignored it.

Mila's hands cupped my jaw, bringing me out of my thoughts. She leaned back to look into my eyes before she brought my mouth to hers for a kiss.

"You're a good man, Grim," she uttered. "I must say that you surprised me."

I kissed the corners of her lips as I brought her closer, molding our bodies together until there was no space between us. The possessiveness and affection that Mila brought out of me was only a testament to how I felt about her.

"You can have me, Mila—all of me." This time when I kissed her, I swooped her up in my arms. I carried her until we were in the bedroom, both undressed, with her stretched out on the bed, and my head between her legs.

Tasting Mila had become an obsession. As she writhed in pleasure, I lapped her essence. Once I was full and drunk off her juices, I kissed my way to her waiting lips. As our lips locked, I rolled onto back, bringing her with me.

Mila wasted no time mounting me. I held onto her titties, squeezing them as her wet, tight tunnel welcomed me. Gritting my teeth through the pleasure, I focused on Mila's face, enjoying the way she bit into her lip, and threw her head back when my head touched her spot. Dropping my hands to her hips, I gripped them as she rode me. Her pussy clamped tight around my length, causing me to grunt.

Sitting up, I licked one of her nipples, then sucked it into mouth. "Sss..." She had me ready to nut and I told her so, spanking her, too, so she'd understand how good she had me feeling.

"Grim!" she cried in ecstasy as she came. Flipping us back over I picked her hips up off the bed and repeatedly drove into her as she came again.

"Shiitt!" I exclaimed, feeling heated all over. Her nails ate at my shoulders. The pain sent me over the edge as I tilted my head back in wonderment. Mila was the only woman who gave me this feeling; the feeling as if I could take off and fly. My soul was surely a part of hers, forming a tie that nothing or no one could ever break. As I emptied my life deep inside of her, I put it on my life that this soul tie was forever.

CHAPTER 8

MILA

The next morning...

Ring!

I stirred as my phone rang, absently wondering who would be calling at this ungodly hour.

"Yeah?"

My heart leapt when Grim picked up the call.

"The fuck you callin' my woman for, nigga?"

Swiftly turning to try and get my phone from him, I met his scowl. The person on the other end must've not responded as Grim disconnected the call.

"Why-"

He kissed the words right off my lips along with the shock spilling from them, then snuggled back under me as he went back to sleep. My mind raced with who could've been on the other end of the line. Anxiety flooded my system.

This sneaking shit was stressful as fuck. Come daylight, it would be over.

Getting prepared to leave was complicated with Grim staring over my shoulder. He was bothered, that much was evident by the set of his dark brown eyes and the lines in his forehead. We'd made love one last time on the deck, not two hours ago. I guess he thought I'd stay a little longer, at least until the sun went down.

But no. I needed to go. I was already near tears from having to leave this man's side. That wasn't good at all. One weekend with a man didn't constitute sadness and definitely not tears.

Lord, and of all men—Grim. The one man I thought would be easy to let go once the weekend was said and done.

"You really gon' leave, huh?" Grim drew from his blunt then blew a cloud of smoke from his nose as he stared at me. He asked me that as if he hadn't just placed my luggage in the trunk of my car.

Heavily sighing, I wished he would just let me drive away without all the drama.

"We've been over this," I said.

Chuckling, he replied, "Yeah, aight."

He waited until I was in my car and driving away before he went back into the house.

As I drove away, I told myself I was leaving Grim and everything we'd done behind. I convinced myself that nothing we did followed me home.

Half-way through my drive with my mind heavily on Grim, I called Kai.

"It took a lot of willpower to not call you, sis," she answered.

Laughing, I said, "I'm teaching you some self-control."

She cackled. "Enough about me..."

Groaning, I replied, "I hate you and Lucy for putting me up to this."

Kai shrieked with laughter. "Yasss! I knew it!"

"Knew what? That his ass was going to ruin me for every nigga I come in contact with?"

That only made her laugh louder. "Hell, yes! Lucy told you not to judge him, boo."

"She did," I admitted begrudgingly.

"Was he such a gentleman that he could, I don't know, actually be your man?"

"Kai," I muttered. "You have no idea." She went to scream again, but I halted her. "However, we agreed nothing would go past today."

"Y'all *agreed,* or you did what Mila does best and didn't entertain the possibility of there being a Grim and Mila?"

Kai knew me so well. "There isn't a possibility. Do you know how bad my anxiety was the entire weekend? My phone rang in the middle of the damn night, and his ass had the nerve to answer it. Who knows who could've been on the other end." The memory settled in the pit of my stomach.

Kai hooted. "See, that's the type of energy you need! One thing about it, Grim is not going to play about you. You saw the way he watched over you at the club."

"He watched over all of us," I corrected.

"No, he didn't," she insisted. "His eyes were on you...the entire night now that I recall." Out of nowhere, Kai gasped. "Oh, this is deeper than what you're saying," she deduced.

I couldn't say anything. Not after Grim confessed his love for me, and not after he'd shown that he cared for me.

"Mila!"

"What am I going to do?" I asked, hoping Kai had the solution.

"Turn yo' ass around and go back to that man," she suggested.

Shaking my head, I replied, "No."

I was already in too deep.

Hours later, I returned from a quick shopping trip, and sulked around my house missing Grim like crazy. Although he'd programmed his number into my phone, I wasn't going to use it. Who would've known that three nights with him would turn into me being so attached to him that I smelled him in every corner of my house, and he'd never been here. It was torture. Torture that I had to endure for two more weeks before he was officially out of my life.

Tomorrow would be the true test. Would I be able to be in the same room as him and not fold? Would everyone look at us and feel our energy knowing we'd been together? The anxiety was overwhelming.

The next morning...

I walked into my office, my eyes immediately falling on the roses sitting on my desk.

Mila,
Our walk on the beach was my favorite.
-Grim

Before I knew it, I laughed. Recalling how he almost had me fighting for my life with those waves made me smile. Grim came across so stern and hood that I didn't know he possessed an ounce of real personality in him, especially not one that drew me in like crazy.

Placing the card on my desk, I reached into my bag and removed the photo I'd framed last night. Smiling, I placed it on my desk. It was a sweet addition next to the roses.

Inhaling and exhaling several times, I gathered up enough courage to leave my office and head to the classroom. Most of my students were already filing in and seated when I waltzed in. I didn't have to look Grim's way to know that he was in his familiar spot, looking, and smelling all sexy. The hair on my body rose to attention as if knowing its owner sat feet away. Suddenly, the skirt and blouse I wore today didn't seem like enough clothes. I felt his eyes touch every inch of my skin, and knowing he'd licked every crevice, I shuddered.

"Hello, everyone," I spoke trying to clear the fog his presence produced. A rumbling of greeting ensued.

The only greeting my ears registered was Grim's, lowly stated, "'Sup, Professor." If I hadn't heard him calling me professor while buried deep inside me, his statement wouldn't have incinerated me the way it did.

Taking a deep breath, I faced my class and prayed I made it through.

Ignoring Grim hurt my heart. I could feel him staring a hole into me, but I looked at everyone but him as I fluently got through my lecture. Not once did I trip over my words or thoughts. I considered it a small fete when class ended, and I hadn't once lost my senses.

I made it through another class before my day ended. Breezing through the halls, strutting like I just won a title match, I was proud of myself for making it through the day. Granted Grim owned my mind but still, I made it. I opened my office door, smiling. My smile swiftly turned into a panicked frown.

"What're you doing in here?"

"I needed to see you," Grim answered. He sat behind my desk, foot perched over his knee, relaxing like this was *his* office. His eyes started from the headwrap I wore and didn't stop until he'd reached my feet.

"You should've made an appointment."

His eyebrows shot up. "I didn't think I needed one."

I stared at Grim unsure of what was going on inside his head. He looked pissed off, so I didn't want to make it worse.

"Last night I watched the video of us in the pool. This mornin' I watched the deck video."

Ooh, what he'd done to me on the deck...I fought a current of heat that surged through me.

"You can't imagine how angry I am with you, Mila." Grim's voice had never sounded so...haunting. At least not when he dealt with me.

"For what? I did nothing wrong."

He chuckled sarcastically. "How much energy does it take for you to lie to yaself?"

I blinked but said nothing.

He motioned to the picture we'd taken on the pier. Now I wished I hadn't placed it there.

"Why is this here?" he questioned.

Going to my desk, I snatched the framed photo up. "Doesn't matter."

Grim tsked. "It matters. If you wanted no memories of me, that picture wouldn't hold a place somewhere that's important to you. You could've left it at ya house. But it's here. Why?"

I refused to tell Grim that the photo was here, on my desk, because it was my way of having him near when I wasn't home. At my house, Grim filled the space because his scent was everywhere. My birthday gifts bore his scent, and so did my clothes.

"Since you won't be honest, I will. We're not over," he drawled. Fatal Attraction real quick

Rolling my eyes at his statement only caused him to utter, "And I mean it."

"I'm not about to be your fuck buddy, Spade. We indulged, it's over."

Grim stood and stalked toward me. As nervous as he made me, I didn't flinch when he brought himself directly in front of me.

"Oh, it's back to that shit now?"

I nodded.

"Hm." He glanced away pensive.

"Exactly. All you want is to fuck me. Why else record what the hell we did? You tricked me into playing your little stupid game."

Grim's expression turned to one of anger as he snarled. "Are you tryna piss me off, Mila? Is that what you want—to see me angry so you can validate why you'on wanna fuck with me?"

"I don't need to validate anything. We're done. There's no need of thinking of a way to change my mind."

He met my gaze.

"The only thing I'm thinkin' 'bout is fuckin' you up for playin' wit' me."

My gaze narrowed on him. "That's the thing; I'm not playing with you, Spade."

His eyes dropped to my center as he neared me. "Call me Spade again," he dared. He stood so close to me, I had to tilt

WTF! I'm sure people can hear

my head back just to keep eye contact. He took the frame from my hand and sat it back on my desk.

My heart quickened from his nearness. Damn, how I wanted everything with Grim. In four days, he'd made me feel shit that scared the hell out of me. I was used to thinking of him as the dog ass man that I believed he was which kept me far away from him. Spending those four days with him proved that there was more beneath Spade Graham than I had ever imagined.

Honestly, I wanted more of him. All of him.

"I see the truth in those beautiful brown eyes," he whispered while backing me up until my butt hit my desk. "Care to act on it?"

I glanced away unable to sustain the heat of his orbs as I gripped my desk for support. He made me so fucking weak.

"Do you want me to lose everything, Grim?"

"Nah, Professor," he said as his fingers skimmed down my arm. "I wanna give you everything. You want me to stop lovin' on you, Mila?"

No!

I hated that my body couldn't reject him in this moment. Nope. Her ass purred like a motor!

"In a few months I'll be a graduate. I hate this sneakin' shit, but I'm sure we can work something out 'til then."

"You make it sound so easy, Grim, when we both know it isn't. What we did this past weekend was perfect. But the reality is that you're you. Grim has never had a kept woman. I'd be risking everything for someone and something that may very well be temporary. Does that make sense to you?"

"Hm," he uttered again.

Thinking he'd drop the issue and leave, I exhaled in relief. Then his hand fell to the swell of my thigh.

"This skirt's got some niggas on my hit list." His hand trailed up my thigh and under my skirt until it rested on my bare ass. "You feel good knowin' you make me homicidal as fuck?"

Eyes wide, I shook my head. Heart tripping in my chest from his touch, I silently begged him to relax.

"Wanting you, all of you, has made me a dangerous man, Mila. I've never felt this shit for any woman. What would you call that feeling?"

I couldn't answer for trying to hold it together as his other hand slid around my throat.

"Does it make sense to you why I just can't walk away?"

He turned me around bringing his length to rest against me. My hands fell to the desk as he unzipped my skirt, sending it pooling around my feet. Instead of protesting and demanding that he leave, I stepped out of the skirt, and parted my legs for him. He pushed me down until my face was planted on the desk.

Gasping as his bulbous head pushed into my wet, tight entrance, I closed my eyes hoping I could ride this out without screaming his name for everyone to hear.

Grim grunted as he sank deeper and gripped my hips for support. His strikes were powerful, sending my vision blurring. Needing to have all of him, I bent all the way over, stifling my moans when he hissed in appreciation. I pushed back, meeting his thrusts.

"Fuck!" he groaned. Glancing over my shoulder I caught the play of emotions on his hard-set face as he sank in and out of me.

He stared into my eyes. "I wanna spank you so bad, baby."

"Mmm," I moaned, biting into my lip to hold back as much as I could as my pussy rippled and vacuumed around him. Squirting on his dick earned me a deep growl that reverberated around my office. My legs shook as he repeatedly hit my spot. Grim held me in place as he viciously pumped into me.

Grim liked to record shit. But I wanted to record this moment in my mind. I dazedly looked back at him. His mouth was agape and his eyes tightly sealed shut. He was so fucking sexy back there, sending me cumming again.

Seconds later, he grunted and stiffened, snarling as he released inside of me. Yanking me up, he kept his pulsing length planted inside of me as he roughly brought my lips to his for a sweet, yet nasty, and rough kiss.

"We're not over," he reiterated.

He left my office with me leaned over my desk spent, confused, and a little scared all at the same time.

That night, I busied myself with whatever I could to keep my mind off Grim. I'd showered, changed into some pajamas, and cooked myself a nice dinner, all with him seemingly clinging to every fabric of me.

Aggravated that his scent wouldn't leave me, I washed my hair thinking that was the culprit. An hour later, Grim's scent still harassed my senses while I stood in the mirror pissed that I had to either straighten my hair or wear it curly. It was already pushing eight o'clock, so straightening it was a hard no.

By the time I slipped into bed, I was so exhausted that I fell right to sleep...with Grim all over me and inside my head.

Thursday arrived and I was so exhausted that I could care less about lecturing anyone. I wanted to get the day over and get home, so I could start my weekend off with a stiff drink. As the thought finished processing, I narrowed my eyes at the person walking into my lecture hall. He was the reason I couldn't sleep.

The audacity of this nigga to be so fine.

"'Sup, Professor?" he spoke.

No smile or anything?

Observing Grim's unbothered expression drove me to wonder if he'd finally came to his senses and realized that he and I couldn't be together.

Great!

Now I could go on with my life as if he'd never kissed me, never held me, or ever made love to me. I'd pretend as if Spade Graham never existed.

CHAPTER 9

GRIM

"Bruh, why the fuck you sittin' there starin' off in space? We need to have you evaluated?"

Cackling ensued as Jacari entered my office with Tito behind him. Despite my depressed mood, I laughed too. It was either that or cuss him out. That would only lead them to dig into my business. My brothers were my heart, and rarely did I come at them sideways about anything. I didn't need them prying into my mind to try to figure out what the hell was wrong with me.

Fuck!

The fact that there was something wrong with me grated my nerve.

"I'm about to get outta here," I answered. I hadn't accomplished one thing tonight anyway.

"Aight; wassup witchu, bruh?" Tito questioned.

Chuckling, I shrugged. "Nothing's up. I'm tired as fuck," I said.

They both shook their heads in protest.

"Nah, something's up," Jacari continued. "I'on give a damn how tired you are, you never leave work behind," he said, pointedly glancing at the unfinished paperwork on my desk.

"Not to mention, it's early as fuck," Tito added.

"This ain't got nothin' to do with Mila, does it?" Jacari badgered. "'Cause you been trippin' since you came from the beach house."

Face screwed up, I asked, "Does tired and Mila sound the same?"

Jacari and Tito busted out laughing. Kain walked into my office shaking his head.

"I'ma start closin' and lockin' my fuckin' door," I grumbled. That only made them laugh harder.

"Even though Jacari's petty as fuck, he ain't lyin'." Kain propped himself on my desk and eyed the stack of paper too. "What happened?"

I thought about not saying shit and just letting them speculate. However, my brothers were married and if anyone understood what the hell I was feeling, it was them.

"I'on understand this woman for shit," I said. "We have chemistry outta this world, but..."

"There should be no 'buts'," Kain answered.

"There's a big ass 'but'," I chuckled. "Her fuckin' job. She ain't tryna fuck with me 'cause of it."

"But you knew that from the jump," Kain stated. "And even then, either she's gon' not give a fuck about her career, or you gon' have to respect her mind. That's what I mean by there shouldn't be any 'buts'. Either she's gon' fuck witchu or she's not."

Being the older brother didn't mean I had all the answers. Especially when it came to shit like love. My brothers found their soul mates and didn't waste any time making them their wives. Me on the other hand, I went all this time in my adult life not seeing any woman as my soul mate.

Now I see how it felt to be *that* man—the man chasing behind a woman. It was frustrating as hell, and frankly, I wasn't built for chasing a woman. Never had. Whatever the fuck changed with Mila, I had to let it go.

Many times, I'd asked myself if I was being selfish, and the answer was always no. Selfish would've been getting her just to mistreat her. That wasn't my intention on any level.

I wasn't sure how I walked into her lecture hall, spoke to her, and pretended like she was just another female, when all

I wanted to do was make my plea for her once more. The look on her face nearly did me in that first day. When I spoke and kept it moving, she looked like she wanted to cry. At least, that's what she looked like to me.

It's been a month now. Mila was no longer my professor, and disappointingly, she didn't once reach out to me. She'd moved into her new position at the university, and because I was such a sap for her, I broke down and sent her roses to congratulate her. The card said nothing other than congratulations, although I wanted to say much more.

I realized that it was deeper than Mila not wanting to jeopardize her career. The bottom line was she didn't trust me, partly because she didn't know me the way she should. Like, the way I knew her. Granted one weekend with me was just that. Yet, I'd shared things with her that I'd dare not share with another woman.

Therein lied what bothered me the fucking most. I let Mila in way before I spent any time with her. Allowing her to own my mind, my soul, and then my body only made me an open book when it came to her. I'ain like that shit.

And then there was my mother, who was on my line every day wondering when the hell she was going to meet her "daughter-in-law". I didn't have the heart to tell her Mila and

I weren't a couple. As far as she was concerned, Mila was just shy.

A knock at my office door drew my attention away from the television screen. I'd been staring at the live footage of the club, supposedly making sure everyone was doing what they were supposed to be doing. It was Friday night, and the club was almost filled to capacity. I wasn't complaining. I just needed to make sure everyone was on their shit. Hell, I wasn't even on my shit.

Nick stuck his head inside. "You want me to handle it, or you got it?"

Confused, I asked, "What?"

He looked at me confused, prompting me to glance at the television. Sharika was at the bar, arguing with Kaleef who was doing his best to ignore her and tend to the guest.

"You got it," I answered.

At a time like this, I didn't need to be anywhere near Sharika. I hadn't fucked a woman since Mila, and I'd be damned if I try and quench my appetite with any woman let alone one that wouldn't understand she was just a fuck.

As soon as Nick closed the door, I buried my face in my hands and scrubbed at my forehead like the action would scrub Mila from my mind. Every night, I went to sleep watching us make love. I memorized the faces and sounds she made. She haunted my fucking dreams, driving me crazy. At this point, I was driving myself crazy.

It was after midnight when I dragged myself in the house, showered, and faced a blunt as I completed a paper that was due Monday. The enthusiasm I normally had when turning in papers wasn't the same knowing it wasn't going to be Mila reading my shit.

Two hours later, I was done and crawling into bed. I purposed in my mind to go to sleep without the assistance of Mila's cries of pleasure.

An hour later, I fitfully reached for the remote to turn on the TV. Mila's beautiful face filled the screen. Her lips were wrapped around my dick, the image on pause because I couldn't handle watching it.

My days and nights seemed to be filled with nothing but thoughts of the woman I wanted more than anything.

MILA

A few days later...

"If you don't throw those things away," Lucy fussed when she entered my living room and saw the vase of wilted roses sitting on my coffee table.

I plucked the vase up, scrunching my nose up at Lucy who shook her head.

"You're hanging on to him anyway you can, and that's pitiful." She propped her hand on her hip and continued to shake her head as I left the living room to take the vase into the kitchen.

Before tossing the once beautiful red bouquet, I took the card from the dilapidated stems for safe keeping.

The note, although simple, meant so much that I damn near cried when I read it. One, because the note was dry with no witty words from Grim. Two, because the note was endearing. While Grim and I weren't interacting with each other, he showed that he still cared about me.

The roses sat on the coffee table for the past few weeks now, reminding me that a man like Grim existed. His arrogance was a true turn-on, and the ease in which he treated me had me sighing for no damn reason.

"It's not pitiful," I defended. "He's actually a nice guy."

Lucy chortled. "Uhm... Didn't Kai and I try to tell you that? Don't make it as if we were the ones telling you to fuck him and dip."

I scoffed.

"That was your decision."

"A decision I had no choice but to make," I said slowly, making sure she understood what I was saying.

She, Kai, and I had been going back and forth about the same subject since I came from the beach house. Kai was disappointed that I didn't at least give Grim a chance to show me that he was worth the sacrifices I was making. Lucy was disappointed that I was being stubborn and not trying to fix the situation.

"Mila, stop lying to yourself," she said. "Nothing terrifies you more than falling in love and realizing that he doesn't feel the same way. Grim isn't Amir. Amir was a piece of shit that attached himself to a beautiful soul just to try and suck the life out of you."

I rolled my eyes as I read Grim's card for the one-hundredth time. "I'm not scared of falling in love," I replied.

"So, you'd rather be in love and not be with him because of your job?"

"Lucy," I admonished. "It's my *career*. I can't just be with a man in some fairy tale life when I have *real* ass bills and responsibilities."

Lucy laughed. "Girl, shut up! You sound so damn selfish!"

"Selfish?" I gasped and looked at Lucy like she was crazy.

She lifted a brow and stared right back at me. "Selfish, Mila. You're saying that you'd choose your career over love.

Grim isn't some man that can't provide for you. He isn't some man that wants to see you lose everything. You've said yourself he's willing to keep everything on the low until he graduates. Still, you choose to choose Mila. For three years you've wanted him. You don't think Kai and I know? We've known which is why we went so hard for you to give him a chance."

Taking the roses out of the vase, I dropped them into the trash can.

"How do you think it makes a man feel to know that a woman he's truly into, would rather have her career, than his love."

"You keep throwing the word love around like you know that's what either of us feel for each other."

Lucy smacked her teeth. "I know exactly what love looks like Mila. The problem is *you* don't."

Damn!

"And don't forget—I know all about sacrifice too."

Lucy's dad was the love of her life. She was a true daddy's girl. That was until she introduced Darren to her father. Her father was against their relationship, and despite his protests, Lucy married Darren. Her father hadn't spoken to her since. However, Lucy and Darren were happily married. Lucy was happy even though she missed her father.

"The baby has you acting mean," I mumbled to break the tension in the room.

She busted out laughing while rubbing her non-existent belly.

"Girl, I'm on Darren's last nerve. If I want him to give me another one, I have to get it together."

Smiling, I said, "I'm happy for you two." I was happy for her and Kai. They were doing exactly what the three of us talked about—the whole marriage and kids thing.

Lucy waved me off. "Doesn't change the fact that you need to really think about this situation with Grim. Do you really want to see him with another woman?"

The thought of Grim kissing and caressing a woman the way he did me burned my skin.

"The look on your face says everything," she chuckled.

Sighing heavily, there was no point in responding to Lucy. Better yet, it was time I looked in the mirror and talked to my damn self. Why allow Grim to own my mind and deny him everything else?

Kai showed up a little while later. Now that I knew they were both pregnant, drinking wasn't something I did around them. Instead, we prepared a simple lunch and sat around the table. They floated baby names around while I sat and listened, fully invested in the conversation although Grim's face slipped in every now and then.

I laughed on cue and added my two cents whenever the time presented. But I didn't know shit about being pregnant or being on this level of happiness and peace that Kai and Lucy were on. I was just along for the ride.

The next afternoon I was in my new office unpacking the few boxes when Mrs. Jackie strolled in.

"Well, this suits you perfectly," she beamed.

Smiling, I replied, "I'm in love already." The office was a little bigger than my other office. The only thing different I planned to put in here was a small sofa. Everything else would look just how it did before.

She chuckled. "Professor Mason says his class misses you."

Snickering as I began filling the bookshelf, I said, "Too bad."

She smiled. "I'm very proud of you, Mila. I've known you since you were a little girl. I remember how much you loved books and pretend playing school with Jodie." Jodie was Mrs. Jackie's daughter. Jodie, too, had a career in education as an elementary school principal.

"Those were the days before we had to deal with the stresses of actually being an educator," I stated.

Mrs. Jackie nodded while cackling. “Precisely, but you handle it well. It’s my honor to have you serving RMU. If you need anything you know where to find me.”

I stopped shelving the books to give Mrs. Jackie a hug. “Thank you,” I whispered.

As she left my office, I thought about Grim. The decision to sleep with him loomed heavily over me. Here I was, accomplishing something amazing, and I’d jeopardized it all for a man.

Something snapped in my brain, bringing me back to something I heard Grim say. He felt jeopardizing everything he’d worked for wasn’t about the money. As long as he protected those he loved nothing else mattered to him.

Lucy was right; did I want to see Grim with someone else? More importantly, was I in love with him? My heart raced finding the truth in the way my heart dropped at the thought of him being in the arms of another woman.

A tap at my door brought me out of my thoughts.

“Yes?” I called.

Professor Sullivan came in, smiling wide.

“Finally caught you,” he said, causing me to snicker.

Ever since my office moved, we hadn’t run into each other.

“Damn, it’s cozy as fuck in here,” he commented.

Observing my new space, I smiled. “It’s okay.”

Professor Sullivan grinned and slid his hands into his pockets. "Congratulations, by the way," he said.

"Thanks, I appreciate it," I smiled.

"So, you and Dr. Jackie are related, huh?"

I paused for a second to glance at him. "No, we're not," I answered and continued placing the last few books on the shelf.

"Oh," he chuckled. "I was passing by and heard her-"

"We're not related," I stated. I automatically knew what he was trying to imply. Professor Sullivan had been with the university for years, and here I came taking a position I was sure he coveted.

"Okay..." He chuckled again. "I'm not saying-"

"So, don't say it. My degrees and experience speak for themselves."

He eyed me with confusion lining his face. "I'm not trying to be funny, Mila."

Maybe I was overreacting. With Grim on my mind, I was a bit anxious.

"Anyway," Sullivan started. "I'm going to miss you being on the same hall as me," he said. He genuinely smiled. "I'll have to find someone else to low-key harass."

I busted out laughing at that. "As long as she doesn't mind," I said.

He snickered and bobbed his head. "See you 'round, Mila."

When he left, I took a deep breath, and relaxed my nerves. I was worked up to the point that I lost interest in unpacking. My eyes fell on the framed photo sitting on my desk. Studying the photo, I took notice of the way Grim's tattooed arms banded around me. Closing my eyes, I remembered how I felt in his arms, as if he was holding me now. I remembered being terrified of heights, until he brought me to the edge, held me, and forced me to see the beauty of the landscape before us. With him surrounding me, promising to protect me, I felt no fear.

I then observed the way my hands rested over his shoulders. One cradled the back of his head, while the other fell around his neck. I clung to him as if I didn't want him to let me go.

Sighing, I blinked away the tears in my eyes and forced myself to finish unpacking.

I had to get over Grim.

The next evening, I stood in front of the full-length mirror in my bathroom, checking myself over once more. Once I was satisfied that I looked decent enough, I left my room, grabbed my purse, and left out the door.

Over an hour later, I pulled into the parking lot of The Code I. I circled the parking lot to check the back of the building to see if Grim's Cadillac was here. I didn't see it parked, so I found a parking spot and decided to wait. All it took was a phone call to know that he'd be at this location tonight. He wasn't expecting me, but I needed to see him.

Last night, I struggled to sleep. This loss of sleep wasn't how it was prior to Grim and I being together. Before, I didn't know what it was like to feel his lips or have him caress me while I was sleeping. Before, I didn't know what it was like to have him wrapped around my body and lightly snoring in my ear. Because I had experienced all of that, letting him go was like cutting off a limb.

Ten minutes passed before my nerves spiked. The source's Cadillac glided into the parking lot and rounded the building. I hadn't experienced an ounce of nervousness until now.

Taking deep steady breaths, I gave myself enough time to make sure Grim was inside.

Once I gathered the courage, I stepped out of my car, and strutted toward the entrance.

CHAPTER 10

GRIM

I had barely sat behind my desk when my office door opened. Nick stuck his head inside.

"I'm about to head to the other spot," he informed me. "Everyone's been briefed for the night."

I nodded my head, rolled up my sleeves then cut the surveillance monitors on.

"Evening," Kiesha said as she breezed in.

"'Sup, cuz?" I spoke.

She smiled and placed a folder in front of me.

"It's officially yours," she beamed with pride.

The property I'd copped from Irv had finally been settled.

"What do you plan on doing with it?"

I shrugged causing Kiesha to chuckle. "Figures," she said while strutting back toward the door.

"Oh! Excuse me."

That voice sent chills down my spine. Mila stood at my door, clad in a black dress that rode her brown thighs the way she rode my dick. The heels on her feet caused my dick to brick up, pissing me off.

"I apologize," Kiesha said to Mila, who was accompanied by Nick. Mila's gaze stayed on Kiesha. The expression upon Mila's face was one I would be concerned about if she was my woman and if Kiesha wasn't family. Kiesha made any woman look at her in disdain. Choppa's wife was built like a brickhouse and loved wearing anything to tastefully flaunt her figure.

"Wanted to make sure she got to you safely," Nick quipped. He chucked the deuces and closed the door.

The door closing brought Mila's eyes to mine.

"Who was she?"

Her question went unanswered.

"Hey," she said visibly nervous.

I didn't speak back. Instead, I coolly assessed her. Mila was the only woman who had the power to bring me to my knees. For that, I had to be careful how I moved when it came to her. Whatever brought her here after all this time could kiss my ass.

Apparently, she heard my thoughts, turning on her heels to leave.

"Yeah, run, shawty," I said to her back, halting her steps.

Whirling back around, she glared at me.

"You act like this is easy being here. Like I'm just supposed to be okay with jumping off a bridge for you, not knowing what waits for me below."

Undaunted, I tilted my head, and asked, "So, why come here? Why risk *everything* to be seen walkin' ya ass into my club, and into my office?"

"You're right." She turned to leave again.

"If you walk out of it, it ain't gon' be open again. You gon' need an appointment, and I may or may not be too fuckin' busy to accept." Boundaries are what I had to set with Mila. She thought she could pop up on my ass just because she wanted to.

She paused in front of the door as I shot daggers at her back.

“Grim,” she uttered. “I need to know I can trust you.”

Trust was something I understood her wanting, but I'd be damned if I let her think she could not have that with me.

"On the pier, the dare, introducin' you to my fam, and every single time you gave me ya body... The night of your birthday... All a part of trust, baby."

Slowly she pivoted on her feet. I rubbed my beard and acted like the tears shimmering in her eyes didn't move me.

"Either you're gon' trust me, or you're not."

"That's all you can say? Grim, you have women at your fingertips. Why do you think it is so easy to trust you? Just because you tell me to?"

"Why be with you if I'ma cheat on you?"

"Says most cheaters," she countered with a sarcastic chuckle.

"Either you're gon' trust me, or there's the door." I wasn't about to play this back-and-forth shit. I had given Mila more leeway than I had ever given anyone. Patience was something she'd taught me to have with her, but that shit was wearing thin.

Standing, I rounded my desk while slipping my hands into my slacks. Her eyes tripped down my body, then came back up, stopping at my lips.

"What's it gon' be, Mila?" I asked stepping into her space. Her breathing changed as my chest connected with her breasts. She smelled so fucking good I wanted to bend her over and make her pay for leaving me.

"Who was she?"

When I didn't answer, she arched her eyebrows, and turned to leave. Before I could stop myself, I was yanking her back my way.

She peered into my eyes, reminding me how easy it was to fall for her ass. I missed her like crazy, but I needed her to come at me correct.

"You once told me that actions speak louder than words. What does me being here say to you?"

I reached up, and ran my fingers through her hair, fisting a handful. She bit into her bottom lip as I grilled her. With my other hand, I took her hand into mine and brought it to my lips. I kissed her palm, then her knuckles.

"Don't you ever call yaself walkin' away from me again," I stated.

"I'm sorry," she tearfully apologized. "I worked hard to be where I am, Grim, and I don't want to disappoint my parents, or ruin my reputation..."

I kissed her juicy lips, silencing her. "I understand ya concerns, love, but I got you. Aight?"

"Alright," she agreed, placing her hands on my jaws and bringing my lips back to hers.

My tongue dove into her mouth, seeking hers. She moaned into my mouth leading me to palm her ass and bring her closer. She knew how I felt about this kissing shit, so she never ceased to kiss me just right.

Moving back toward my desk, I brought her to sit with me.

"Lemme handle a few things, so we can get outta here," I said.

"Of course," she replied. She made herself comfortable atop my lap, placing her head on my shoulder and closing her eyes. Chuckling, I made do, and handled my business.

Hours later, I parked in my garage and cut the engine. Mila stirred, stretching her body like a cat. I softly grabbed her chin and kissed her lips.

"We're home," I said.

Her eyes popped open, quickly glancing around.

"This doesn't look like the beach house," she mentioned.

"It isn't," I confirmed.

Getting out of the car, I went to her side, and opened the door.

"Where's my car?" she asked as I helped her out.

I pointed to my left. Her car was parked in my garage also, having been dropped off earlier.

"You fell asleep in my arms," I chuckled.

She snickered. "Sorry about that. Haven't had much rest."

Reading between the lines, I quipped, "You gon' get plenty of rest here."

Smiling, she let me take her hand. I led her inside the house, with her admiring everything her eyes touched.

"I thought I was in love with the beach house. This...this is breathtaking," she admonished. She stood at the patio door overlooking the backyard. It stretched far and wide.

"May I?" she asked. Nodding, I unlocked the door, then slid it open.

She stepped onto the deck, mouth ajar in fascination.

"Grim!" she gushed. "This is absolutely amazing." Her face tilted toward the starlit sky as a wide smile graced her face.

"If I lived here, I'd never want to be anywhere else," she said.

"Not even the beach house?" I chuckled.

She shook her head. "This is the type of environment for a family, raising kids..."

Her words trailed off as my arms went around her waist.

"You talkin' about family and kids like that's what you want," I uttered in her ear. She shivered against my body.

"I-I..." she stuttered. My lips touched her neck, while my dick poked her ass, making it impossible for her to form any thoughts.

"As much as I tried to stop, I watch us every night. I'm addicted to you like a muhfucka, Mila."

She shifted in my arms, turning to meet my feverish gaze.

"Baby," she whispered, while stroking my beard. "If you're addicted to me, why aren't you inside of me yet?"

I took her ass in a rough kiss and groaned as I lifted her off her feet. Her heels hit the deck on a thud as her legs went around my waist. Nothing was gentle about the way I sucked and bit on her as I carried her back into the house. The nearest piece of furniture is where I deposited her.

The straps holding up her dress fell down her shoulders, hanging on for dear life, and exposing her beautiful globes. Mila's swollen lips puckered as she wantonly squeezed her titties and pinched her nipples.

Hurriedly, I stripped, not caring about anything other than being deep inside her walls. Naked, I snatched her to the edge of the sofa and pushed her dress up. Seeing that she had no panties on, I mugged her.

Whatever was on my lips died when she reached for my dick, fisting me. Quickly, I freed her of her dress and reveled at her beautiful body while pushing into her wet tunnel.

Damn. Her tightness fucked my head up along with the sounds she made the deeper I sank.

"Oohh," she purred as her silky walls hugged me.

I positioned her knees over my shoulders, needing to be as deep as possible. Gritting my teeth, I forced myself to try and relax, but being back inside of her had me lit.

With her legs over my shoulders, I palmed her titties, and slowly moved inside of her.

"Ssss..." I hissed, then attacked her nipple, sucking it until she started writhing beneath me.

"Griimm," she moaned palming my head as my pace increased. "Please!" she begged.

Grunting, I dipped deeper, calling her name when she gripped me so tight I nearly busted.

"Fuck!" she shouted, coming undone.

As her body shook with the force of the orgasm overtaking her, I threw my head back, and continued stroking her through it, dying from how good she felt melting around me.

The pleasure was too much, though. I missed her too much, *needed* her too fucking much.

"Mila!" I growled when she started cumming again. Although I wasn't recording this moment, everything about what Mila did to me, and what I did to her branded itself on my brain.

Fuck! I was in love. As I pumped my life into her, I repeatedly chanted her name, and at the same time I dared her to try and pull some fuck shit again.

*****

Our first date was at Choppa's restaurant in downtown Pensacola. It was risky, but Mila was excited to finally go on a real date with me. Choppa arranged for us to have a private dinner, which made it even better.

During dinner, Mila's genuine laughter drew me in deeper, making me realize that I was right in being in love with her. She smiled whenever her parents came up in a conversation, and even said that she couldn't wait for me to meet them.

I mirrored her emotions, letting her know that my parents were just as eager to meet her. Replaying what happened with my mother the night of her birthday had Mila rolling with laughter.

"I still can't believe you pulled that off," she'd said.

"Anything for you," was my response. It rendered her speechless.

Throughout the rest of dinner, she blushed whenever our eyes locked. Her pureness and confidence once again had me in its grips. There was something about being in the presence of the one you knew would be yours forever.

Mila's eyes lifted, staring into my soul. She must've read my thoughts, because the smile she gave me, was full of love.

"I'm so in love with this place," Mila said a few nights later as we lay upon a comforter, underneath the starry sky.

"How much in love?" I asked, snuggling her closer.

She smiled against my chest.

"I don't ever want to leave," she voiced.

"Then don't."

*****

MILA

I bobbed my head to a Mariah Carey song as I tapped at my keyboard. My spirit was high off the night I'd had with my man, hell, the past two weeks I'd had with my man.

Grim had me in a state of bliss that only a grown man could bring a woman. He catered to me in ways I had only ever imagined. And the fact that he did so because he wanted to caused the smirk on my face to grow into a full smile.

The last two weeks had been the best of my life. Grim and I were so close, it felt like we'd known each other for ages.

"Knock, knock!" My mother's voice jarred me out of my thoughts.

"Mama!" I shrieked, jumping from my desk to hug her.

Laughing, she embraced me just as tightly. I hadn't seen her since the weekend after my birthday.

"I thought I'd pop in and invite you to lunch," she said.

"Yes, of course!" I went back to my desk to close my computer and retrieve my purse.

"The pictures don't do your office justice," she admired, glancing around in approval. Her eyes roamed my office until they fell on the frame holding the picture of me and Grim.

"Who's-"

"Hello!"

My heart stopped in my chest.

Grim strolled into my office looking delicious as fuck in black slacks and a black button down. I stared at his freshly lined, bearded face as if I didn't wake up with it planted between my thighs this morning. He licked his lips, echoing my thoughts as he gave me a quick once over.

The outfit I had on matched his. He'd gotten me dressed this morning. The thought made my face burn.

"Hello," my mother spoke, smiling in Grim's face.

My heart was pounding, unsure of why Grim thought this shit was funny. Of course, he'd never met my parents, but he'd seen them on photos.

"I'm Spade," he introduced and shook my mother's hand. "Let me guess—Mrs. Dash?"

Mama grinned as heat entered her cheeks.

"Why yes," she answered, flustered.

"It's nice to meet you. No wonder ya daughter is so beautiful; the two of you are twins," he noted.

Clearing my throat as it felt constricted, I stretched my eyes at Grim while my mother drank in all his charm.

What the hell are you doing?

"I was on my way to see Professor Mason," he said, answering my question. "I hope you and your daughter have a beautiful day."

He gave me a smirk before leaving.

"Wow!" Mama exclaimed under her breath.

I was still trying to regulate my heartrate.

"What?" I questioned.

"You work with him?" she quizzed.

Shaking my head, I replied, "No. He's a student from the class I taught."

Mama's head snapped back.

"Student? That man looks like a-"

"Ugh, mama, no," I chuckled. I did not need her take on my man.

"What?" she innocently asked. "I was just going to say he's handsome."

"Hm, hm," I said while ushering her out of my office.

Glancing down the hall I caught Grim's back. Sensing me staring he peered over his shoulder and shot me a smile. Although I wanted to cuss him out, all I could do was smile on the inside. Because on the. inside, I was dancing like a love-struck girl.

Through lunch, I listened to my mother laugh about something crazy my dad had done. Truthfully, I wasn't laughing at their foolishness, but rather Grim's. Sometimes it scared me thinking about how easily I'd fallen in love with him. I had known since the night of my birthday. Grim went out of his way to see to my happiness. So, no matter that thoughts circulated in my mind to be careful, I couldn't. The craziness of falling in love so deep and so soon was lost on my fool's heart.

"Mila!"

"Huh?" I met my mother's concerned expression with one of my own.

"Are you listening?" she queried.

"Of course!" I faked.

She continued talking with me drowning her out once more.

CHAPTER 11

MILA

Lucy and Kai laughed so loud half the store turned to see what was so funny.

"He did what?" Lucy balled over with laughter.

"While y'all are laughing, I was sweating bullets while he stood there smiling all up in my mama's face."

Kai hollered. "His ass is crazy!"

"I tried to tell y'all he was fucking crazy," I fussed.

I pushed my cart past them as they continued to laugh at my expense. Telling them what Grim did yesterday was not so they could clown about it. I wanted them to see what they'd gotten me into, *who* they got me involved with.

"How cute though," Lucy sighed.

I turned my nose up. "Cute?"

"Yes, cute. That man wanted to meet, mama," she explained.

Come to think about it...

"His boldness alone is so damn sexy," Kai added.

His boldness was wha attracted me to him in the first place.

"Okay, listen," I said gathering their attention. "I'm not sure if it's the baby hormones or what, but both of y'all fail to see the point."

Lucy clucked her teeth. "We see the point, sis. We had to *force* you to be with a man that makes you happy."

"Regardless of what you say, Grim meeting mama made you smile," Kai said.

I did not respond or else it would've been a lie.

"You have us tagging along, so you can make your man the perfect dinner tonight. Don't tell us you don't feel a way about Grim. It's perfectly fine for you to feel how you want to feel," Lucy voiced.

"That's just it," I sighed. Grim catered to me often, spoiling me. Tonight, I planned to have dinner ready for him by the time he made it home. Lucy and Kai were here to assist me as I hadn't cooked for a man in forever.

"Mila!"

Swiftly the hair on my neck stood to attention, and not in a good way.

"Is that Amir?" Kai barked. Her hands flew to her hips while Lucy dug in her purse for her phone, presumably to call Darren.

Amir stalked towards us mugging me.

Why is this nigga popping up now! Fearful, I started to panic.

"Come any closer, I'ma shoot yo' ass," Kai threatened.

Amir thought twice, until Kai produced a gun.

"You know who my man is, so you know my aim is on point," she warned.

Amir leered at me before backing away.

"Baby!" Lucy was speaking to Darren on her phone.

"No," I begged before she could say anything.

Confused, she stuttered over her words, then told Darren she'd call him back.

"Girl what the fuck is wrong with you?" Lucy asked.

Upset and ready to leave the store, I headed right for the checkout. "I don't want Darren getting involved and before you ask, you already know why."

Darren and Chuck would kill Amir. Even though he was on some creep shit popping up on me, I didn't want him being killed because of it.

"The fuck did he even find me?" I questioned aloud.

"Maybe he followed your mom," Kai fumed. "That makes the most sense."

If that was the case, then I was going to have to nip this shit in the bud. I wasn't going to walk around being afraid of Amir. As long as he thought I was afraid, he would keep doing the dumb shit he was doing.

That evening as I prepared dinner for Grim, the events of earlier kept clouding my mind. Every other second, I was looking over my shoulder, leading me to become even more upset.

Once Lucy and Kai made sure that I got to Grim's safely, they lectured me about dealing with Amir before things went any worse than they already had. I swore them to secrecy, but I felt bad for putting them in a position where they couldn't be honest with their husbands.

There had to be some reason why Amir was back on my case. Niggas like him moved on with another woman just to use her a placeholder for the woman he still wanted. Once that woman realized what she was dealing with and let his ass go, he goes and tries to disrupt the life of the woman he truly wanted. The cycle was vicious and unnecessary.

Amir wasn't about to do that to me, though. I'd found peace, happiness, and the love of my life. No one was taking that from me.

"Baby girl." Grim's voice never ceased to move me. He entered the kitchen, grinning. The gift bag he carried drew my attention.

"Hey, baby," I spoke.

Grim placed the bag on the table and moved toward me.

"The food is ready, I'm about to make your plate-"

A kiss to my lips silenced me.

"'Sup?" he asked enveloping me in his arms. Grim looked at me strangely, before kissing my lips again. I prayed Lucy nor Kai said anything about earlier.

"Nothing's up," I denied.

"Hmmm... I beg to differ." He tilted my head back until he stared into my eyes. Him studying me so closely made me gulp. I felt his lips, then his hand left my throat.

"I'ma go shower. You comin'?"

Shaking my head, I replied, "I already did."

Grim smoothed his hand over his beard, amused. "Aight," he said and left the kitchen.

I went back to fixing his plate, thinking about what the hell I was going to do about Amir. One thing was for sure—he wasn't about to come in and disrupt my life. Sighing, I carried Grim's plate over to the table.

"Whatever's on ya mind, don't let it get you fucked up."

Startled, I almost dropped the plate.

"Nothing's-"

"You would've been asked me what's in the bag or at least tried to look in it," he stated.

The gift bag sat in the same spot on the counter where he'd left it. Now that I looked at it, the bag was the same we'd gotten the day on the pier.

"Like I said—don't let it get you fucked up." Grim left the kitchen with me following his retreating frame.

*****

Monday morning started off hectic. With classes almost complete, students and faculty alike were stressed out, and stressing each other out.

Aside from work, Grim and I were the same other than the fact that he was subtly trying to pick my brain about what my issue was. As we got ready this morning, he assisted me with wrapping my hair in the new headwrap he'd purchased me, and casually brought up what it was like to not know a person's thoughts.

"Shit is frustrating," he'd said.

All I did was sigh and pretend like the statement wasn't directed toward me. Grim was so attentive that him recognizing something was wrong with me wasn't a surprise. In fact, I loved that about him.

I opened email after email, rifling through shit that made no sense. It occurred to me that I missed Grim's emails. Now that we were together, I had him at my fingertips.

Still...

Grim: Need anything before I leave campus, baby?

Me: No. I miss you.

Grim: Leave early and meet me at home.

Me: Can't. Tons of work to do.

I rolled my eyes at the last part. Although I loved my role, it came with its headaches.

Grim: Aight. Hmu if you need me. Otherwise, call me when you leave, and I'll meet you at home.

Me: Okay, boo.

I smiled and placed my phone on my desk, eager to get the day over just so I could see Grim's face. It didn't matter how much I crowded his space, he always welcomed me. A few nights he'd be in his home office working late. I'd take my lonely ass in there and climb in his lap. Instead of pushing me away, he'd make room for me, and continue working as if my grown ass wasn't snoring in his ear.

So, yes, Grim had me spoiled rotten. I loved it.

A few hours later the day was finally starting to wind down when Sullivan appeared at my door.

"Hey," he spoke. "I just wanted to come by and--"

"Excuse me," Mrs. Jackie interrupted as she entered my office behind Sullivan.

His eyebrows peaked as he observed Mrs. Jackie's expression.

"I'll...uhm, come back a little later," he said and left.

"Mila," she called. Her usual smile wasn't upon her face. She quietly peered around my office until her eyes met mine.

"Somethings come to the board's attention," she said, causing my heart to stall. I didn't like how this sounded already.

"We received information alleging that you've been engaging in a relationship with a student," she explained.

Feigning shock, I said, "That can't be." It couldn't be, because Grim and I had been careful. Even when we went out, we went to places that were secluded. For the most part, we stayed home and found other ways to enjoy each other. Grim made it known that he was tired of us sneaking around, but that as long as we were together, he'd make do. Graduation wouldn't come soon enough.

"The board has launched an investigation into the allegations. If proof is presented and you're found to be guilty, the university will have no choice but to fire you."

Fear sliced through me. Here was the anvil coming down on my head.

"I've been advised to have you placed on administrative leave. Once the investigation is complete, should all be found well, you will be reinstated."

Blinking back tears, I said, "This can't be happening,"

Mrs. Jackie sighed. "Honestly, I don't believe any of it. However, we must follow protocol. I didn't want anyone else informing you which is why I'm here. Everything will be kept close to the vest until all the facts are gathered."

Nodding, I croaked, "I can't believe this."

"It's okay, Mila. We'll get to the bottom of it."

Yes, they would. That's what scared me. My mind raced as I gathered my purse and important belongings, before following Mrs. Jackie out of my office. The only people on my mind right now were my parents.

As my phone trilled with a call from Grim, I didn't answer it as I drove toward Mobile. The fact that I couldn't cry about this burned me. Because it was my own fault. There was no one to blame but myself.

*****

GRIM

Me: Where you at, baby?

I'd already called Mila twice, and now she wasn't responding to my messages. According to the time, she should've been off an hour ago. Figuring she was in the middle of something, I didn't worry. Yet, a minute later, I picked my phone up just to verify she hadn't responded yet. My eyebrows crinkled together just as I did start to worry.

"Everything good?" Kain asked.

I was at The Code II having a drink, chilling with him and Choppa until Mila got off.

"I'on know," I absently replied.

Ten minutes and another phone call later, I saw Lucy and Kai stalking my way.

Hours later, I was at The Code II having a drink and blunt with my brothers when Lucy and Kai sashayed into the club. Mila wasn't with them, which made me stand, concerned.

"'Sup?" I asked. They both looked upset.

"Someone reported Mila to the university's board."

Shit!

"Where is she?" I questioned even as I attempted to call her again.

"Her parents' house," Kai answered, then recited the address.

Lucy sighed heavily. "Her ass should've told you about Amir."

My head snapped up in the middle of me typing the address into my phone.

"What the fuck about that nigga?" I felt my lip curling up and my blood boiling which wasn't a good thing.

Both hesitated to say anything until Darren's loud outburst had his wife jumping, startled by his thundering voice.

"The hell you ignorin' my calls for?" He approached his wife who hurried up and tried to explain.

"Bae, I was trying to handle something with Mila."

Seconds later, Chuck walked into the club, his eyes immediately falling on his wife.

Kai turned to me and groaned. "We were grocery shopping the other day when Amir popped up. He...uhm..." She glanced at her husband who tilted his head.

"He what?" Chuck demanded to know.

“Mila didn’t want anyone to know that Amir’s been stalking her, alright,” Lucy explained.

“So, when he approached us, I pulled my gun on him, so he’d leave,” Kai finished, nervously chewing on her lip as she gave Chuck puppy eyes.

“We think he’s the reason Mila’s in trouble,” Lucy concluded.

Silence followed their admission as Chuck and Darren assessed their wives. Leaving them to deal with their issues, I dialed Mila again while heading toward the exit.

“I’m behind you,” Kain said. I nodded

It’d been a while since I bodied a nigga. Twice now I had allowed Amir to slide—once at the wedding two years ago, and the night he called Mila’s phone. I wasn’t giving him anymore passes.

Fuck that.

*****

On the Dash’s street, I crept up the quiet, suburban road, observing the lone car parked alongside the curb of Mila's parents' house.

Amir was so fucking stupid his dumb ass didn’t think anything of it when I parked behind him.

Kain shook his head and chuckled. “I swear, some niggas deserve to be fucked up for the shit they do.”

I concurred. Stepping out of my car, I left my heat tucked and casually walked up to the driver side window.

Drunk, Amir didn’t see me because he was too busy crying and singing a Dru Hill joint. He went to lift the bottle of brown to his lips when I snatched it out of his hand.

“The fuck!” he exclaimed.

I snatched him through the window, then sent his head through the back passenger window.

“Ahh!” he screamed in pain. Bloodied, he held his face and cried harder.

“What the fuck, mane?” he whimpered in pain. “What I do?”

“You fuckin’ with my woman!” I barked. Amir tried blocking my fist busting his head open, but I was too quick and too lethal for him. Amir hit the ground in a heap.

“Grim!”

Mila’s footsteps clapped against the ground as she ran toward me. Her voice didn’t deter me from pulling my gun and pointing it at Amir’s head.

“Grim!” she yelled in fear.

Baby girl had never seen me like this. This man that loved and doted on her was a whole killer outchea. I hated she had to witness this side of me. It was only a matter of time.

"Do something!" she begged Kain, who was propped against the hood of my car watching like this was an everyday occurrence for us. Shit at one point we'd been in the trenches, handling shit this very way.

Meanwhile, Amir held his hands up, eyes wide as he began to hyperventilate.

"No, mane! I'ain do shit! I swear I'ain touch her!" he professed.

Face screwed up and finger on the trigger, I stared right into Amir's fear-filled eyes.

Mila appeared at my side, frantic.

"Please, Grim," she reached for my hand holding the gun. "He isn't worth this. Please—I need you," she stated tearfully.

Snapping out of my rage, I lowered my gun. Never did I leave a man alive after I'd gotten this far. Niggas loved to seek revenge, and I had no time for that bullshit.

"What the fuck is going on?" Mr. Dash came down the driveway, a nine at his side.

"Is that Amir?" Mrs. Dash was right behind her husband.

Mila grew more anxious as they approached. Kain came over to peel a whimpering and bloodied Amir off the ground.

"Spade?" Mrs. Dash gasped.

Tucking my gun in my back, I let Kain handle Amir while I addressed Mila's parents.

"I apologize, Mr. Dash. I hate that we're meeting under these circumstances." I offered my hand, which he shook. "Spade."

Mrs. Dash was stuck on mute as she glanced back and forth between me and Mila.

"Nice to meet you, I guess. You whooped that nigga's ass, so we're good," Mr. Dash said.

"*Why* did he whoop his ass, though?" Mrs. Dash questioned.

"Dad, mom, go back inside," Mila suggested to her parents. Reluctantly, they started walking back toward the house.

"You go inside too," I said to her.

"I'm not going inside until you come with me." She folded her arms over her breast and poked her hip out.

"Gon' on," Kain seconded. "I'll handle him." He'd already placed Amir's dizzy ass back into his car and shut the door.

"What're you going to do to him?" Mila asked, panicking again.

"Does it matter?" I quipped.

"Yes, it does," she shot back. "Not because I care about him. I care about you, and this," she motioned to Amir, "can get you in a lot of trouble."

Chuckling, I replied, "This ain't nothin', sweetheart. A nigga come for you, he's comin' for me."

"Yes, but-"

"Ain't no fuckin' buts!" It came out as a growl, startling her. "Shit, my fault, baby." I brought her stiff body into my arms and kissed her forehead. "Listen, I'ma go handle this. I'll be back and we can talk."

She wanted to protest, but the look on my face had her pivoting on her feet. She glanced back a couple of times; concern set in her face.

I climbed into the driver's seat of Amir's car and pulled away from the curb. Kain followed me.

CHAPTER 12

MILA

I walked into the house, praying that Grim wasn't about to kill Amir. Amir was a lot of things, and deserved to get beat up, but killing him was pushing it. Grim revealing that side of himself had me both intrigued and scared as fuck.

The tattoo on his make made sense now. Grim's expression had been the one mirrored in the tattoo. Shaking my head in denial, I sat on the couch and pretended not to feel the daggers my parents shot my way.

After leaving the campus, I shot straight here to cry on my mother's shoulder. My tears had nothing to do with Grim and everything to do with whoever stooped so low to try and bring me down. There was only three weeks left until graduation. Grim and I were right on the cusp of making it through without getting caught.

No, what I was doing wasn't right. But when it came to Grim, my sacrifice didn't seem much at all. Plopping down on the couch, I buried my face in my hands, exhausted by the day's events.

"So, it's true?" My dad uttered after a few minutes had passed.

"Daddy," I went to try and explain. "I can't explain it, alright?"

They studied me. As much as I was concerned about how they would react, I was more concerned about Grim. I'd been ignoring his phone calls and messages, trying to sort out my thoughts and how I was going to get out of this mess that I was in.

In no way was I about to go down without a fight. Sure, I was in the wrong. However, there had to be some way I could fight this.

"What you're saying, is that you and Spade are..."

Nodding, I met my mother's gaze head on. She could be mad about me risking my career over a man, but I wasn't ashamed of Grim. Even if I'd just witnessed him about to take someone's life.

Lord.

What was wrong with me that Grim being so crazy turned me into liquid? Knowing my man was equal parts teddy bear and savage stirred my middle. I had to fan myself from the heat of seeing him with his lip curled up.

"Yes, mama," I answered.

"The day he introduced himself, were you two together then?" she questioned.

I confirmed with a brisk nod.

"He looks familiar," daddy said.

"He's Darren's cousin," I explained. Darren's family had some of the same features.

"Oh," they replied in unison.

Mama smoothed her hands over her hair, then came and sat next to me.

"Now things make sense," she mumbled.

Lifting my brows in question, I wondered what she was talking about.

"You've been happy...so to speak," she hesitantly stated.

My neck slightly snapped back, shocked. "I'm always happy, mama."

"Not like this," she chuckled.

Unapologetic, she hunched her shoulders. "What was I to think? We figured at some point you'd tell us you were dating again. We didn't want to be in your business."

While I appreciated the fact that they respected my boundaries, they were taking things too well.

"Aren't you upset?" I glanced back and forth between them, curiously wondering *why* they were taking things so well.

"Your mama and I were once in your situation, Mila," my dad divulged.

My mouth dropped.

"We've been working together for years, dear," my mother replied. "When we first started dating, fraternization was frowned upon. We did so much sneaking just so we could be together." She laughed while reminiscing. "Jackie is the one who talked me into being with your dad in the first place."

I knew a lot about how my parents met, however, these details were certainly left out.

"But you two still work for the same school. What made them okay with it?"

"You did," daddy answered.

"When I found out I was pregnant with you, we decided it was the perfect time for me to stop working. I stayed home my entire pregnancy, during which time, your dad and I got married. Once you were old enough to walk, I went back to work."

"So, here I am hiding everything from the two of you for no reason?"

They chuckled.

"I think he's a great young man," my dad said.

"You've only known him for a split second, daddy."

"But in that split second, he tore Amir's ass a new one. Speaking of that situation."

"Oh, Lord," I grumbled.

"Oh, Lord, nothing," mama sassed. "Has he been following you?"

"He was harmless at first," I explained.

"Mila," daddy griped.

"I know," I sighed. "I just didn't want you to kill him for doing the petty things that he was doing."

Daddy guffawed. "I'm the least of Amir's worries at this point."

His statement only made me drop my head back into my hands. Grim was somewhere out there "handling" business, while I sat here wondering what the hell all of that entailed. My day had started great, and now I was jobless, with a man that was undoubtedly every bit of the beast he displayed this evening.

"What am I going to do?" I wondered aloud.

Mama's arm went around my shoulders. "You're going to wait right here for him. When you get home, you're going to prepare him a nice dinner, and be ready to both talk and listen."

"He clearly cares about you if what we witnessed says anything," daddy added.

What I witnessed was scary as hell. Amir's ass had better be thankful that I cared about Grim enough to stop him. Shuddering at what could've happened had I not been there, I went back to worrying about Grim and where he was.

*****

GRIM

"I'm sorry, mane," Amir repeatedly mumbled.

"I'ain tryna hear that bullshit," I informed him.

"I'ain do nothin' to her. I just miss her, mane." He busted out crying and tried to reach for the liquor bottle that had fallen on the floorboard. When I rounded a curb, he leaned against the door, dazed.

"I'on give a fuck 'bout that, nigga. You just like every other muhfucka who learned too late what the fuck they had. That don't mean you go fuck with her, or the next nigga she got. 'Specially if her nigga is anything like me."

"She's a good woman, mane. You'on understand." His garbled response made me grill him.

"Nah, *you* didn't understand. You outchea tryna ruin her career and shit 'cause you in ya fuckin' feelings. You a grown ass fuckin' man actin' like a bitch."

"What?" he mumbled, confused. "I'd never ruin Mila. I just wanted her to talk to me. She up and left me like I wasn't shit."

I pulled over into an open field and cut the engine. Regarding Amir, I replayed what he'd said.

"You've been followin' her all this time," I said.

"No, I haven't," he denied. "I had a girl, mane. We broke up 'cause I couldn't stop talkin' about Mila. I followed her mama the other day. Until then, I didn't know she worked there."

Exhaling a deep breath, my mind shifted to other more capable muhfuckas who could've ratted out my woman.

"I'd advise you not to drive while you're drunk," I told Amir, then slipped from the driver's seat.

His eyes grew as he surveyed his surroundings.

"Wait, mane! You can't leave me here!"

His pleas fell on deaf ears as I trekked to my car, where Kain was waiting. I slipped into the passenger seat and accepted the blunt and lighter he handed me.

"You leavin' that nigga outchea with Jeepers Creepers," Kain noted.

Laughing, I stated, "He better off outchea than with me."

"Most definitely," Kain agreed.

We made it back to the Dash's a little while later. I sent Kain back to Pensacola and would drive Mila's car back home. I spent a few minutes talking to her parents. Just so Mila and I could get back home, I agreed to treat them to dinner this weekend.

"Did you kill him?" Mila asked. The car had been quiet until then.

We were on the highway headed back to Pensacola. Although I was upset that she chose to run to her parents instead of me, I squeezed her thick thigh.

Glancing from the road to peek at her, I said, "Nah."

She looked away. "Then why were you gone so long?"

My hand left her thigh to tug her chin until she was facing me. Dividing my attention between her and the road, I replied, "If I killed that nigga, I would've been straight up about it. Don't disrespect me like I'd ever lie to you."

"I'm not disrespecting you. Who would own up to killing someone, Grim?"

"I would—to you."

"Oh, really?" she asked skeptically.

"Yeah," I answered. "If a man got a woman that's real and down for him, he'll share anything with her. She becomes his confidant. He's the most vulnerable with her, 'cause he can trust her. I'ma be honest; you runnin' up here rather than comin' to me has me feeling some type of way."

"Why? They're my parents. If anyone understood how I was feeling, it's them."

"Wow, aight," I chuckled.

As much as it stung, I had to respect her mind. I took my hand from her thigh and rested it on the gearshift. Mila was starting to make me rethink what the fuck I was doing...again. I wasn't this nigga. Cutting people off was my strong suit. So, why the fuck couldn't I cut off Mila? She had me stuck on her ass.

"I'm sorry, Grim. Please don't take it the wrong way. You are special to me-"

"I can't be," I interjected. "I told you before actions speak louder than words. If I was *special,* I would've been ya first call. I damn sure wouldn't be ignorin' ya fuckin' calls and messages." I was getting angrier.

"You're taking it the wrong way," she reasoned, reaching for my hand she brought it to her lap. "You *are* special to me. I... I just needed some time to think. Me being at my parents had nothing to do with me not needing you."

I begged to differ.

"Even if my actions sometimes confuse you, they're never against you. I'm with you because I want to be with you. If that means moving on from my position, then I will. I told you that I need you. I mean it."

The car remained quiet the rest of the way home. When I parked in the driveway, I cut the engine, then checked on Kain, Jacari, and Tito.

"Tell me what's on your mind, Grim. This silence isn't like you."

"Actually, it is," I stated as I responded to my brothers' texts. "You've just never had to deal with this side of me. I'm a man that's used to havin' my way at all times. With you, I'm playin' ya fuckin' game, going by ya fuckin' rules. I'm makin' every effort to be the nigga you need and deserve. If you can't reciprocate my energy, then why the fuck are we together? Sad part about it is, no one's ever had Spade before, except my mama. I keep tryna give him to you, but you act like he ain't just as important as Grim."

One minute I was replying to a text from my mama, and the next, Mila was in my lap ripping my phone from my hand. She glanced at the screen, then finished my text before tossing the phone to the passenger seat.

Her arms went around my shoulders as she straddled me. Ignoring how her pussy rubbed against my dick was futile. He stood to attention, ready for war. I licked my lips in need while she gulped.

"I need you," she whispered. "I need Spade Grim Graham. I love your smile, and the way you bite your lip when you're inside of me. I love your mind, and the way you speak it at will. I love the smell of you, and what it does to me whenever you're near me."

My dick clung to the sound of her low, sultry voice, growing to the point I had to adjust Mila's position. Just this morning I was sucking on her clit and eating her pussy so good she barely made it to work. Recalling her flavor, I licked my lips again.

"Ooo..." she moaned when she sat on him. She leaned forward and kissed my lips. "You forgive me, baby? Never will I doubt who you are to me, and what place you have in my life. It no longer matters what I have, as long as we're together."

This time when she kissed me, her tongue made it past my lips. I palmed her ass when her hips moved against me. Just as quickly she opened the car door and got out. I took her proffered hand and stepped from the car.

I smoothed my fingers over my beard as I walked behind her and watched the bounce of her thick ass. As soon as I had the door opened, I wrapped my arm around her waist and walked her left, toward the den.

Within seconds I had her clothes off with her ass in the air, and her head buried in the sofa as my swollen head penetrated her sex.

"Ohhh!" she gasped.

I pushed deeper, gritting my teeth against the pleasure. The stretch marks lining her ass had me so fucking in love. Once I was fully seated, my hands smoothed over the deadly arch she had in her back. The action caused her to contract around my shaft.

"Shiiitt!" Slowly I slid in and out of her tight wetness, nose flaring as her juices stained my dick. I caught my bottom lip and groaned every time she hugged me.

Mila's fingers gripped the couch for support as she sniffled and moaned in ecstasy. I sped up catching her as she threw her ass back. Her pussy rippled around me, curling my toes.

"Cum, baby," I encouraged, hitting her deep. Without hesitation, she created a vice grip around me and exploded on a broken cry.

Pulling out, I flipped her onto her back and entered her. I sucked her right nipple as I beat on her spot, loving the way she sexily screamed while scraping up my back. I felt her coming again, driving me to push her thighs back and steadily ride her through it.

“Griimm!” she shouted.

It was her face and the grip of her pussy that sent me over.

“Quit fuckin’ playin’ wit’ me,” I growled in her ear. Seizing her mouth in a delicious kiss, that sealed everything I felt for this woman. “I love you,” I confessed while staring into her watery eyes. Seconds later, I exploded inside of her.

This bitch needs a pregnancy test ASAP!

CHAPTER 13

GRIM

Two nights later...

Sullivan's house was in downtown Pensacola, amongst the area known as the historic district. His house was all brick, encompassed two floors, and had a shed out back in the small lot his house sat on. Like the rest of the houses on the block, his was neatly kept.

I made quick work of breaking into his shit. First, I found his security system which, not surprisingly, wasn't on. Some people thought because they lived in a 'good' neighborhood' shit wouldn't happen to their property.

I shrugged and chuckled when his computer didn't have a password and let me right in.

"Stupid nigga," I mumbled. It only took a few minutes to delete what he did have recorded. Once I was sure the system was disabled, I carefully made my way through the cleanly kept house.

Nothing looked out if place and was too clean as if no one even lived here. I went into every room, looking for anything that could clue me in on this nigga. He was surely the person responsible for Mila being under investigation. I needed something to prove it. The last room down the upstairs hallway was the last to check. I twisted to the doorknob to find it locked.

Recalling that none of the other doors in the house had been locked my gloved hand twisted the knob. Hell, his computer didn't even have a code on it, but *this* door was locked.

Within seconds I had it open, stepping into what appeared to be a darkroom. All the windows were covered, leaving the room pitch black. I cut the light on and growled at what met me.

Thirty minutes later, Sullivan twisted the doorknob to enter the room, whistling a tune as he flicked the lights on. His eyes bugged at the sight of me.

"Is that my woman's pussy and my dick plastered all over ya fuckin' wall?"

Sullivan's Adam's apple bobbed, his fear evident.

"How did you get in my house? I'm calling the cops."

"I'll do you one better."

I grabbed Sullivan by his throat and smashed his head on the wooden tabletop, then kneed him in his stomach sending him balling over.

"Ahhh!" he screamed.

I put him in a chokehold, squeezing, wanting to snap his damn neck.

"Who the fuck you think I am, nigga?"

He couldn't answer for the hold I had on him. He clawed at my arm, but I was too strong for the likes of him. For this reason; I dressed in all-black, from my head to my fingertips and toes. The nine made it effortless for me to get him tied to the raggedy ass chair positioned behind an equally raggedy desk.

"Please," he cried. "I'll do anything."

"Yeen gotta do shit but sit there and shut the fuck up."

Taking one of the washcloths laying across the table, I blindfolded him causing him to cry like a bitch.

"Kinda pervert ass shit you got goin on in here?" The photos of me and Mila were taken in her office leading me to concur that he'd been recording her. "From the looks of it, there's dozens of different women in these photos, all of whom are naked and unaware they've been photographed or recorded."

"Please," he mumbled through his snot and tears.

"What's funny is that I should hide you for this. Seeing as how you caused a lil' ruckus at my woman's job, it'll look a lil suspicious if ya ass comes up missin'."

He cried harder.

Me: I need a cleanup.

The burner phone was only used in times like this. I dropped the address and got a reply within a minute.

CC: OTW

Sighing, I looked around the room again, shaking my head in disgust.

"Sadly, this shit would've never gotten out if you hadn't fucked with my woman."

"I'm sorry," he whimpered.

"Nah, yeen sorry yet."

Ten minutes later, Choppa, Nick, and Kiesha strolled into the room, confusion lining each of their faces. They were expecting a body. I placed my finger over my lips and pointed to the pics of me and Mila.

"Sweep the whole fuckin' house and the shed; leave no trace."

Nodding, they got to it without any other instructions. My crew knew if it involved me, the entire premises had to be swept cleaner than a muhfucka.

"Who's that? Who's in my house?" Sullivan panicked.

"Don't worry," I assured him. "They're helping you out. You know how many felonies you're looking at, Sully? I think I spotted some underage-"

"No!" he shouted.

"Yeah, I did," I replied.

"Please," he begged. "I'll never survive in prison. Please just kill me," he sobbed.

I chuckled. "Thing is, I love torture. I love watching people suffer, especially if they've crossed me in any way. You crossed me in the worst way."

He whimpered loudly.

"Therefore, you gotta suffer. While I hate that it won't be at my hand, I love that it'll be at the hands of dozens of niggas who can't wait to meet you."

He broke out crying, causing the crew to snicker as they did their job scrubbing any evidence of me and Mila away.

I paced the floor contemplating my next move. I'd never doubted killing someone that really deserved that shit. Sullivan needed to suffer for the things he'd done, but by my hand would bring heat on me if he'd already shared our photos.

"Stupid bitch should've never took what was mine."

I stopped in my tracks and realized Sullivan was no longer crying. Instead, a sinister smirk was plastered across his face.

"It's always the sistas that gotta come in and take over what belongs to a black man. I wanted to bury her ass for taking my position. Her and that bitch Mrs. Jackie can go to hell." He chuckled.

Three pairs of eyes followed me through the room as I spotted a rope sticking from under his desk. Several hooks hang from the ceiling, none strong enough to hold his weight. There was one, however, that stood out. It was attached to a chain that was bolted into the ceiling. There was no telling what he did with that shit.

Grabbing the rope, I swiftly looped it around Sullivan's neck. He bucked in fear. Choppa untied his legs and helped me hoist him up while Nick dragged the chair over to the area where I was about to hang this nigga.

"I'm givin' you what you want," I told Sullivan when he cried in fear.

"Noo!" he screamed.

Thanks to him and his weird obsession, his padded and blacked-out room made it to where no one could hear him. With little effort we got him in position, then sat his feet on the chair. The crew left me with Sullivan and went to sweep the rest of the house.

"Who did you report Mila to?" I questioned.

"He's on the board. Michael," he wept.

"Where's the video you gave him?"

"I didn't give him shit!" he wailed. "All I wanted was for her to be investigated. I never planned to substantiate anything. Do you know how it would look if I showed them my..."

Kissing my teeth, I said, "Yeah; it's gon' look crazy as fuck."

He sniffled as I rounded him.

"Prison or hell?" I offered.

"Wh-what?" he stuttered.

"You heard me the first time."

"B-but... I can't..."

I tipped the chair back and let it fall to the floor. Sullivan writhed like a fish, causing me to smile. I removed the blindfold so that he could look into my eyes.

"You're sick," I said to his distorted face and bugged eyes. I removed the cloth from around his wrists. His hands immediately flew to the rope, clawing at it. "Imagine what everyone will think when they see ya little playroom. Why you got all these fuckin' ropes in here? How many women have you hang from this hook? Imagine what everyone will think when they see ya lil' playroom. Trust me... Hell is better."

Sullivan’s body stopped writhing as the rope choked his airway. His arms fell to his sides. For a minute, I just stood there, staring into his lifeless eyes, cocking my head at him in shame.

*****

MILA

Nervously, I chewed on my manicured nail while waiting for Grim. My parents and I were already seated and served our drinks, but Grim hadn’t shown yet. With the way my anxiety had been over the last couple of days, I expected him to beat us to Choppa’s restaurant.

I was partly nervous because Grim told me that he loved and I’d yet to echo his feelings although I felt the same. I was afraid that he’d only said it because we were making love at the time. I waited patiently for him to repeat his words, but I hadn’t heard him say it sense.

“Relax, baby girl. He’ll be here,” my dad said bringing me back to the matter at hand.

The only reason Grim and I didn’t ride together was because he had a last-minute meeting. Just as I was thinking we should’ve rescheduled, he breezed into the private room looking sexy as hell in gray slacks, and teal button down. A gift bag dangled from his fingers as he sailed toward us.

We stood to welcome him, with him first, wrapping me in his arms.

"Hey, baby," he stated and kissed my lips. "I apologize I'm runnin' late."

Shooing away his apology, I wiped my gloss off his lips and smiled. He hugged my mom and shook my dad's hand before we all sat. Nosey, I glanced at the gift bag. Grim always had a way of slipping me gifts, however, this bag was free of a logo and unfamiliar to me. He chuckled.

"Let's order our food and talk," he suggested.

Impatiently, I sat through waiting for our food, Grim and my parents talking about everything from sports to children and how many Grim wanted. His ass gave them an answer, surprising me. They congratulated him on the success of his businesses and his pending graduation. As Grim's woman, I was proud of him.

Dinner went well. My parents were no doubt in love with Grim and he genuinely liked them as well. We were standing to leave when Grim reached for the gift bag.

"Oh, yeah. Let's gon' and handle this," he said.

Confused, my face wrinkled up.

Reaching inside the bag, Grim pulled out a small square gift box. My mother gasped and so did I. Grim dropped to one knee and took my left hand into his.

"I love you," he said.

Tears sprang to my eyes as I rapidly blinked, thinking this was a dream.

"I love you so much, I need you to be mine forever. Will you do that for me, Mila? Will you marry me?"

Dropping to my knees in front of him, I cupped his face and stared into his eyes.

"I love you," I choked out. "And yes, I will marry you."

Grim slid the beautiful diamond ring onto my left ring finger. The beauty of it stunned me speechless. My parents clapped and cried with me as Grim lifted me off my feet in a tight hug. When he kissed me, nothing else in my life mattered.

The shower we enjoyed together was full of deep grunts and screaming. I sucked Grim into a trance before he put me against the shower wall and reminded me who was running the show.

He was. And I was going to let him.

*****

Today was a strange one for the students at RMU. Those who were graduating were excited for the next chapter in their lives, while others were too busy focused on the gossip going around campus.

Several days ago, news broke that Professor Sullivan committed suicide in his home. Although the police were remaining tight-lipped, several people heard that Professor Sullivan had been into some weird things. Not only that, but a few female students began coming out about how Professor Sullivan treated them. They claimed he was bribing women into sex. The thought turned my stomach. Then I recalled what he'd said in my office about finding someone else to harass.

I shook my head and prayed none of these women had been on the receiving end of anything traumatizing. Seeing all their beautiful faces smiling and glowing as they crossed the stage brought back my own memories from graduation. I remembered it like it was yesterday and all the hard work I'd put into making it that far. I'd accomplished so much in such a short time.

The board had yet to enlighten me on my suspension or my position with the school. There wasn't a day that passed that I didn't think about being in my office or standing in front of a classroom. I felt like it was truly my calling.

However, as my man's name was called over the speakers, I beamed with pride and clapped for him as he strutted his fine ass across that stage. I didn't give a damn how many women whistled at him, he was mine and I'd be sitting on that fine ass face and big dick he carried around for decades to come.

Fanning myself, I pulled my mind out of the gutter and watched the rest of the ceremony.

An hour later, I ran toward Grim, who was surrounded by his family, and jumped into his arms. He caught me with ease and planted a kiss on my lips.

"Congratulations!" I shouted with tears in my eyes. "I'm so proud of you, baby!" He wiped them then kissed me again.

"Thank you, beautiful," he smiled. Although I was still wrapped around his body, he introduced me to his parents and his brother's wives who were all gorgeous.

"This is my fiancé, Mila," he said to his parents.

Their mouths dropped.

Deciding I needed to have a little class, I had Grim place me on my feet so that I could properly meet them.

"It's nice to meet you," I said with my hand stuck out. I yelped when Grim's mother snatched me into a tight hug.

"Baabbyyy! Thank you, Lord!" she exclaimed causing everyone to chuckle.

Mr. Graham hugged me as well and welcomed me to the family. I went back into Grim's arms and held on tight. As he rocked me, my eyes met Mrs. Jackie's. She was walking by hand in hand with her husband. A smile played along her lips, then she dipped her head in a nod. I smiled back, grateful that she understood.

married, cant fire me

EPILOGUE

MILA

The wind whipped my hair as I slowly rode Grim to the backdrop of the waves crashing on shore. Underneath the thick blanket our bodies flowed together just like a smooth current. Tilting my head toward the stars, I tried focusing on them through my blurry vision. But as Grim sucked on my budded nipples, I closed my eyes and begged him not to stop.

"I'll never stop lovin' on you, baby," he promised.

He'd never stopped thus far. It was August now and we were stronger than ever. We'd scheduled our wedding for December and would have it in Miami. Everyone was excited, including the two of us.

"You feel so good," I moaned into his mouth. My walls were fragile these days, quivering so hard around him that I couldn't stop from cumming if I wanted to. I had nagging suspicion that we had a baby on deck, seeing as I hadn't had a cycle in over a month just after I'd stopped taking my birth control. The decision had been both of ours after Grim brought it to my attention. I was all too eager to follow my man's lead.

He hit me deep, causing me to gasp as my head tilted back even more.

"Ya beautiful ass. I can't wait 'til you're carryin' my name and my seed. I swear on my life I got us forever."

My pussy gripped him hard, sending us both over the edge. We fell back on the blanket and smothered each other in a wet kiss. Grim pulled the blanket up to shield our bodies against the wind as we laid here for a few more minutes. I was in the arms of a man who loved me unconditionally and treated me like the shit I'd read in stories.

It took weeks for the board to close the investigation into the allegations someone reported. Mrs. Jackie smiled with pride as she'd given me my position back. While I was happy, risking everything for Grim turned out to be the best thing I could've ever done. What I got in place of what I thought I had was true love.

GRIM

Life was great. Business was great. Shit was just great. A nigga didn't have one complaint—not when I had the love of my life in my arms.

Holding Mila would never get old. When I held her, I made sure she felt like a queen in my arms. I kissed along her neck and cheek, marveling at her beauty.

Every now and then she and I would watch the videos of us making love, just because. Even then, the love shown through our eyes, and the way we carefully, yet savagely pleased each other.

"The water is beautiful today," she commented.

We stood on the pier, overlooking the water as we'd done countless times before. The sun was bright in the sky, bouncing off of Mila's glorious skin the same way it shown over the water. The gentle breeze reflected my mood. I was content, at peace, and happy as fuck.

Soon, Mila would be my wife. She carried my baby in her womb, growing the best parts of us so beautifully that it brought me to tears whenever I felt our love move inside of her.

"You're beautiful, my professor," I told her.

She snickered. Her hand came up to cup my jaw. "Thank you, my love. I love you."

Smiling, that was one of the many things I didn't question when it came to us. Mila loved me to no end. She showed it in the way she kissed me, the way she smiled at me, the way she stared at me when she thought I wasn't looking. She showed it in the way she rubbed my beard, the way she laid under me, and the way she made love to me. She showed me that she loved me. The best part of all, she showed it in the way she let me lead without question.

She was my professor, my woman, my love until we both took our last breath. Sneaking with her was easily the best shit that ever happened to me.

THE END

BOOKS BY M. MONIQUE

A Thug Has Feelings Too

A Hitta Has Feelings Too

A Baller Has Feelings Too

A Hitta Has Feelings Too Part 1&2

Heart of A Champion Soul of A Boss

The Illest: A Gangsta's Holiday Love

Anything Necessary For Her

Falling For His Savage Ways

Painlessly In Love

Healing A Gangsta's Heart

Friend U Can Keep

Whisper A Promise

Uncovering Love

Blu

A Goon For Christmas

Kingston

The Bridge

Sneakin' & Freakin With My Professor

ALSO AVAILABLE

ALSO AVAILABLE

ALSO AVAILABLE

ALSO AVAILABLE

ALSO AVAILABLE

ALSO AVAILABLE

ALSO AVAILABLE

ALSO AVAILABLE

AJPRESENTS

PUBLISH YOUR BOOK WITH US!!!

For submissions, please send us:

A query letter, a one-page synopsis of your story, and the first three chapters of your novel or the first fifty pages, whichever is more. If you are submitting your novella manuscript, please ensure it is between 17,000 and 40,000 words. In all other respects, please follow the standard manuscript formatting guidelines.

Please remove all running headers, footers, illustrations, images, and special type from your submission. We are best able to assess work that is formatted simply, according to the guidelines below.

Please be aware, too, that we are unable (given the number of submissions we receive) to provide manuscript feedback to individual authors who do not intend on being published by our company.

We only accept electronic submissions via email.

AJDAVIDSONPUBLISHING@GMAIL.COM

"I write for my people..."
I write because I love sentences
and I love freedom more."

Imani Perry
2022 National Book Award
for Nonfiction

Made in United States
North Haven, CT
16 September 2022

24201010R00139